# VIVA LAS BAD BOYS!

# VIVA LAS BAD BOYS!

HelenKay Dimon

BRAVA

KENSINGTON PUBLISHING CORP.
http://www.kensingtonbooks.com

BRAVA BOOKS are published by

Kensington Publishing Corp.
850 Third Avenue
New York, NY 10022



All Kensington titles, imprints and distributed lines are available at special quantity discounts for bulk purchases for sales promotion, premiums, fund-raising, educational or institutional use.

Special book excerpts or customized printings can also be created to fit specific needs. For details, write or phone the office of the Kensington Special Sales Manager: Kensington Publishing Corp., 850 Third Avenue, New York, NY 10022. Attn. Special Sales Department. Phone: 1-800-221-2647.



ISBN 0-7582-1476-6

First Kensington Trade Paperback Printing: August 2006
10 9 8 7 6 5 4 3 2 1

Printed in the United States of America

To my mom, Joan Dimon, who taught me a love of reading and an appreciation for books.

To my dad, Scott Dimon, who never complained about the cost of those books, or of the tendency of the females in the household to buy them with an almost scary abandon.

Thank you both for your love and support.

Acknowledgments

You probably know Las Vegas is real. The people in this book—no. The situations—no. The Berkley Hotel and Casino—no. The blackout—yes. So, for the spark of an idea and, yes, even for the unexpected blackout, I owe a special thank you to the wonderful staff at Bellagio. You made a multi-day power outage bearable.

Authors often refer to writing as a lonely and solitary process. For me, that's not quite true. The process started with an editor who trusted me enough to buy a book based on a six-line pitch: thank you, Kate Duffy. Continued with a critique partner and dear friend who kept me on track and made every page sound better: thank you, Wendy Duren. And ended with a husband who tolerated vacation and quality time interruptions in order to support my deadline: thank you, James. I couldn't do this without all of you.

*Contents*

# JACKPOT

# Chapter One

"Feeling lucky?"

Jack MacAllister smiled at his companion of one hour. "I'm not a great believer in luck."

"Better not let the Vegas tourism folks hear you say that or you'll have a date with a bus going straight out of town."

Actually, his only date for the evening had been a blackjack table. Until she sat down. A sexy blonde blessed with a sweet round face and the husky voice of a telephone sex operator. The same woman wearing a big white wedding dress.

A rule probably existed somewhere that said harmless flirting was not so harmless if the woman in question happened to be a bride. Someone else's, that is. But he wasn't ready to believe this one even was a bride. Something about this lady's story didn't fit. The attitude, the lack of excitement. The absence of a groom . . .

If she weren't so damn sexy, he'd run for cover in any direction that included a bar. But that wasn't happening.

About fifteen minutes ago she'd looked up at the big screen television in the nearby betting area and started spewing out college football statistics. Exactly ten seconds after that he'd fallen deep into lust. His ass hadn't moved since. If there was anything hotter than a woman who knew about sports, well, he didn't know what it could be.

When she moved to the rows and rows of shiny, flashing slot machines and asked him to join her, he did. He even kept up the pretense of polite conversation by wasting a hundred dollars in less than fifteen minutes on slot play.

After all that time watching her, he still didn't know her story. He knew how her shoulder-length hair bounced against her slim shoulders when she laughed. He knew how her grass green eyes sparkled with excitement when the reels rolled her way. He knew because his sorry ass had been stuck on the same uncomfortable stool forever watching her nurse a twenty-dollar bill and eighty credits.

But her wedding? The groom? Nothing. Not one word.

She didn't strike him as an obsessive nutcase who liked to dress up in fancy gowns for fun. Of course, she didn't strike him as a woman celebrating the best day of her life either.

She said something, but he lost the thread when a group of what could only be described as Beautiful People stepped out of the Berkley Hotel and Casino elevators squealing at a decibel level he'd bet would shatter glass. The women, all with straight hair and even straighter bodies, headed for one of the many bars outlining the gambling area.

"Very pretty. Your type?" She did some shouting of her own to be heard over all that giggling.

"They look hungry to me."

"Haven't you heard? Thin is in."

His gaze returned to his companion and wandered over her petite frame. She was compact, with full, high breasts. Even under the sharp yellow lighting he could see the healthy glow to her skin.

"Where do women get this crap?" he asked.

"From other women."

"You're not going to blame men, the media and the evils of advertising?"

"There's enough blame to go around, but women are the worst." She looked past him. "Speaking of blame."

He looked over just in time to see a tourist dragging a suitcase the size of a coffee table slam into a tall, useless-looking guy in a tux. Casino employees dressed in burgundy blazers swarmed the scene.

"That can't be good for business," she said.

"Alex has it under control." A low rumble of background noise filled the air as men and women puffed on cigarettes and grabbed up free booze as if security guards weren't engaged in the equivalent of international peace talks in the middle of the floor.

"Who?"

He shrugged. "Alex Mitchell. The assistant manager."

She shrugged right back in an exaggerated style that made him laugh. "You visit enough to be on a first-name basis with the guy who runs this place?"

"Let's just say Alex is the type to give a personal welcome to frequent guests."

"Ahh, I get it. You're a high roller."

"I come here whenever I need to clear my head." Time to steer the conversation to neutral ground. She didn't need to know about the size of his bank account or the huge decision facing him back at the office. "With the new construction, the shutting down of part of the pool deck and all the other inconveniences that go along with expansion, Alex is doing everything he can to keep the patrons happy."

"What construction?"

Not the most observant woman he'd ever met but certainly one of the more attractive. The kind of attractive that translated just as well in the bedroom as in every other room of the house.

"You didn't notice the second tower going up right behind this one? The big crane?"

"Uh, no."

"Guess you prefer indoor activities." He loved those types of activities.

A bell started dinging behind him, reminding him there were a few things about Las Vegas he didn't love. Things he actually hated. Specifically, slot machines. He despised all that ringing and shrieking whenever anyone won a measly ten bucks.

"Maybe we should try another game. One that actually requires a level of skill higher than picking lottery numbers," he said.

"This machine is going to hit."

Since her eyes sparkled with hope, he almost hated to shoot her down with the truth. He tried anyway. "I hope you're kidding."

"No, really, I can feel it. Gambling isn't usually my thing—"

"So, naturally, you came to Vegas."

She ignored him and rambled on. "I've been within inches of hitting progressive a few times." She pointed at the screen. "I just need the circle with the big B to land on the line next time. It was just below the line last spin."

Great. A novice. "You know it doesn't work like that, right? It's all chance. There's no skill involved. What happens one spin has no bearing on what happens the next. It's all based on a series of numbers—"

"Stop."

"But—"

"I'm as fiscally responsible as the next person. More so, really, but this is different. Don't ruin my fun." She had one hand wrapped around the neck of a beer bottle and the other gripping the slot pull as if she'd fall through the floor without the thing to support her.

"You're right. I'm sure you're within inches of lifetime financial security."

"That's better."

"And, you don't have to pull the lever. It's for show only. Just push this," he said, pointing to the "spin" button in front of her.

"I like the feel of the stick."

Of course she did.

He swallowed down something that tasted a bit like lust. "Far be it from me to ruin your day with a little realism."

"Good man." She gulped back a mouthful of beer.

If she was going to pickle herself, he should at least have some biographical information to tell the ambulance crew. "You still haven't told me where your groom is."

She stopped in midswig. "You didn't ask."

Oh, he was sure he had. Twice. In between the part where he imagined her wearing skimpy pastel lingerie and the part where he peeled them off her inch by mind-blowing inch. She'd ducked the question both times.

"Yeah, well, I'm asking now," he said.

"Don't know, but if I had to guess, I'd say somewhere with his hand up June Peters' skirt." She set the bottle down with a clunk and pulled on the handle, sending the slot reels spinning again.

"Is that in a code only those without the Y chromosome can understand?"

"What?" she shouted over the newest screaming frenzy happening in the row behind them.

Maybe talking slower would help. "June Peters is . . . ?"

"Was."

"Damn. Is she dead?" He hoped not, since it sounded as if someone was busy fondling her.

"Of course not."

"Fine, I'll bite. June Peters was . . . ?"

Her hand dropped from the pull, and she stared, the full force of those intense eyes right on him. "My best friend, marriage witness and maid of honor. The same June Peters who slept with my fiancé yesterday."

Maybe the bride thing wasn't a sham after all. "Oh," he said because nothing else seemed appropriate.

"Yeah, oh."

"So, when did you find out?"

"About two seconds before I hunted down one of these women carrying around the liquor and ordered the equivalent of a case of free beer."

Probably what he would do. Right after he beat the hell out of someone. "Sounds like as good a plan as any."

"It's my only plan."

"I guess you didn't get married."

"Why would I marry a man who cheated on the eve of my wedding?"

"I have no idea why women do anything." Or men, for that matter. Hell, he didn't believe in lying either, but that seemed to be how everyone he trusted treated him lately.

"Not married." Her eyes narrowed a bit. "And you?"

"Single. Not so much as a tan line." He held up his hand and wiggled his fingers as evidence.

"You're, what, forty-five and still single?"

"I'm thirty-five, but thanks for overshooting by a decade," he said.

"That young? Really?"

"So, did you actually see which way that liquor woman went? I have a sudden need for an extra large Tanqueray and tonic with a beer chaser."

"Sorry." She said it, but the chuckle suggested she didn't mean it. "I'm terrible with ages." She crossed her legs, sending a bolt of fabric drifting off to the side and exposing a mile or two of toned thigh and calf, along with strappy white heels.

"There's terrible and then there's insulting," he grumbled under his breath.

"So, you don't have a wife, you wear nice clothes, you

have a designer watch and you haven't moved from that seat in forever."

He tried to pull his gaze away from her legs, but that task proved harder than expected. "I'm quite the catch."

"You're interesting." That perfectly sculpted leg started swinging back and forth. "So, anything else a woman should know about you?"

How about that bride or not, he was ten seconds from stripping that damn dress right off her. The neckline scooped low enough that the job would take only a tug or two. "You hit the highlights."

"Nothing else, then."

Nothing he felt like sharing. Nothing he could share with a stranger or even a friend. "Nope."

"How about your name?"

Ah, yes. That. Names were good. Names meant progress and possibly a move upstairs. He hadn't come to town looking for a one-night stand but wouldn't refuse the opportunity. Not now. Not when everything at work was in an uproar. Not when he needed a release.

Not when he wanted to see what game this lady was playing.

"Jack. You?"

"Laine. As in Elaine, but don't call me that unless you want to breathe out of your armpit."

"Elaine is a nice name."

"Don't make me get off this stool."

"Warning received." Sexy and sharp. If Laine did have a newly former fiancé, he ranked as one of the biggest dumbasses of all time.

"Good thing because I'd hate to have to hurt you."

"Yet, you sound happy about the idea."

She exhaled, and miles of creamy skin pressed against the top of the lacy gown. "So, we have an understanding."

If that was code for foreplay, then, yes, they understood each other just fine. "Where's the hubby-who-almost-was right now? Just want to know in case he decides to pop up and beg for forgiveness or something."

"If we're lucky, he's under a bus."

"Ouch." Maybe taking a furious woman to bed wasn't such a great idea after all.

"More like thank you," she said with a huge grin. "June did me a favor."

She didn't sound heartbroken. Good thing because weepy women were a personal no-no. "How's that, exactly?"

"Now I can enjoy Vegas."

*Green light.* He leaned forward, letting her soft fragrance drift around him. "You know, Laine, I just might be the man to help you with that."

She snorted. "Is that a line?"

Oh, yeah, he definitely needed more liquor. A new move might not be a bad idea either. He slid back on the uncomfortable stool and signaled for the cocktail waitress to bring him a big glass of something dark and unholy.

"Admittedly that wasn't my best work. Maybe the dry air is throwing me off," he blustered his way through the ego beating. "I might need to reassess my strategy."

"No need. It works for you somehow."

"Now, be careful. That almost sounded like a compliment," he said. "And, despite what you might think, the offer was genuine."

"Genuine?"

"As real as that diamond on your finger." The same one with the cheap, fake, out-of-a-gumball-machine look to it.

He got the reaction he wanted. A look of surprise flashed across her face, then vanished as quickly as it appeared. More clues. Still no answer as to her identity or the origin of the fluffy dress, but there would be time for that later. Like postbed and preshower.

"Are you from here, Jack?"

"Just visiting." The words rushed out a bit faster than he intended.

Her full lips hovered just inches above his. "Relax, Jack. Forget the dress. I'm not looking for a commitment."

"I'm not offering."

"First names. Fun only. Walk away without regrets."

Sounded like the perfect relationship to him. "We can use code names if you prefer. You be Natasha. I'll be Boris."

"Jack and Laine are fine."

He planned to take her from fine to climax within the half hour. "Then we're agreed."

"Yes."

"Would you like to go upstairs? You know, so you can change," he asked, hoping she could catch a line when a guy threw one right at her.

"Subtle, Jack."

"I thought the dress might be . . . itchy."

"It scares you."

Hell, yeah. "Let's just say there's something about a wedding dress that makes a man a little—"

"I believe the word you're looking for might be itchy."

"Exactly." He waited a beat or two. No need to look desperate. "Let's go."

She scooted off the stool and tucked her arm under his, pressing her ample breasts against his chest. With her hand on his forearm, she walked beside him. He could feel the warmth of her slight touch through his Egyptian cotton shirt.

"Your room," she said.

He looked down and waited for her to finish. She didn't disappoint him.

"I'm in the bridal suite."

He tripped on the straight carpet. "Forget that."

"Exactly. My room has memories. Yours doesn't."

Made sense. His lower half sure thought it sounded good. "What about changing into other clothes?"

"Jack, honey, for what I have planned we won't need clothes."

# Chapter Two

About time the man showed an interest in something other than blackjack. For a supposed womanizer and big-time drinker, Jack hadn't engaged in much of either over the last two days. She knew because she'd been following him around, trying not to nod off from boredom.

Then she'd moved to a new tactic. Instead of following him, join him. She, Laine Monroe, former desk jockey, had ramped up her pseudo-surveillance.

The gown was supposed to be cover. She'd paid a real bride, one who'd said she was on her fourth marriage, fifty bucks to borrow it until morning. The lady wanted the gown back in its protective bag and with her luggage when she left the hotel to go home. Guess she thought she might need it for a fifth time.

That gave Laine about twelve hours to play fantasy bride and get what she needed. And, really, who knew a wedding gown would work like an aphrodisiac. Jack had leapt at the thing as though it were made of chocolate. Proving, once again, men were as unpredictable as injured animals.

"You okay?" He asked the question as they stepped past the casino security guard and into the private elevator to the exclusive upper floors.

"Do I look something other than okay?"

"Delicious, maybe?" He leaned back against the mirrored wall and brought her knuckles to his mouth for a quick hot kiss. "Taste it, too. But, it kind of kills a guy's ego to have you frown when you're walking to his hotel room."

Maybe he was a player after all. "A sensitive issue, huh?"

"Let's just say we're touchy about things like women frowning, crying or making any other negative sounds or gestures when heading for bed."

"I'd think doing those things *after* would be the real problem."

"Thank you so much for putting that worry in my head. I thought we would just have a good time. Now I know to expect a grade."

"I'm sure you'll be great."

"This is starting to feel like kindergarten." His tongue tickled the crevices between her fingers, then smoothed over her knuckles.

Her brain waves scrambled until she couldn't remember her name. Who knew such a kiss would be so damn sexy? "So, you did this kind of thing at age five?"

He pressed her back into the glass. "I was always a bit advanced for my age." He whispered each word against her lips on a soft puff of air.

"I can see where that would be true." She could see everything. This close, his ocean blue eyes lit with fire bursts of green, and soft flecks of blond highlighted his light brown hair. His firm chin, high cheekbones and sly smile were nearly irresistible.

Shame she wasn't really there for the sex.

But she was rethinking her priorities with each passing second.

He nuzzled his nose against hers and hummed the tune playing in the background. Something escaped her lips, but it didn't rise to the level of being an actual word. More like a sigh with a hint of a groan.

"We're here." As soon as he said the words, the elevator glided to a smooth stop, and the doors opened.

"Quick ride." That fact ticked her off. "Sinatra didn't get to finish his song. I was enjoying the show."

"Mine or his?" He pointed up to the speakers.

"Yes."

He pressed his palm against the small of her back and guided her down the long, wide hallway. "I guess this is one of those times scientific ingenuity is not a good thing."

"I always hated science." Loved math. Like, her plus him equaled electricity. Yeah, she got that equation.

"The good news is that the same song is likely to be playing on the elevator tomorrow around this time."

"Convenient." His earthy male scent, a mixture of musk and a crisp fall morning, tickled her senses.

Her floor had a classy yellow and green décor. His made hers look like a campground. With the super private goons guarding the place, the fortieth floor defined lush. The thick carpet squished beneath her two-inch heels. Any other time, she'd be barefoot and sinking her toes into the soft pile.

Now wasn't the time. She was on a job. Sure, a job no one had hired her to do, but still a job she took seriously. Operation Compromise Jack MacAllister. She needed proof. Needed to know what Jack was doing and what information he had in his hotel room. Which was why she needed to get in there.

This wasn't about her. This was about one of her former clients. About owing him. She refused to fail a second time. Failure had never been an option in her life. Now it was all she did.

Jack brought her to a stop in front of a set of double doors. "We're here."

She stared at the tiny green light and keypad to the right of the wide opening. "What's with all the bells and whistles?"

"It's a combination doorbell and message center. It looks impressive but malfunctioned earlier, so I'm not convinced it's such a great idea."

He acted as if every room in the hotel had these extras. Not exactly. Her standard room thirty-eight floors down didn't even have an ice bucket. The one treat she did have was the ability to purchase tap water in a fancy bottle for ten dollars a shot.

"Does Alex know about this technological travesty?"

She was joking, but he took the question seriously. "I told him."

"Uh-huh. So, are you expecting a lot of guests with a lot of messages?"

"Not unless your bridal party is meeting us later." He tapped his key card against the door. "Is there a problem with my room?"

"Other than the questionable waste of money?"

His face went blank. "You lost me."

"Really, Jack, there are better uses for your monthly income. Investments. T-bills. Tax-free bonds. Unless you're using this trip as a write-off, I'd say this is a waste."

He frowned at her. "You sound like my financial planner."

With good reason. Her other life, the old one, had taken over for a second. "Well, you should listen to your finance person. This isn't a reasonable expense. This isn't normal."

"The 'this' in that sentence would be?"

"A big ole suite the size of my house."

His blue eyes stared right through her. "As opposed to the bridal suite you're staying in."

*Busted*. "Uh, what?"

"Did you analyze all the financial angles when you planned your wedding at a swank Las Vegas hotel and picked that room?"

"Of course not. Weddings are romantic, not . . ." Her brain stopped functioning. Not what?

"Mathematical?" He leaned against the doorjamb and crossed one ankle over the other. "See, I'd think the bridal suite would be pretty plush, it being the nicest room in the casino and all."

"Sure." She figured a short agreement made the most sense here.

"Probably a bigger waste of money than my room," he pointed out.

"Uh, yeah." She tugged on her ear, hoping the move would jump-start her sleeping brain cells and stop her from saying "uh" a hundred more times.

"Anything you want to tell me?"

He looked so approachable and open that she almost told him. Almost came clean and asked him straight out. But if Mark's suspicions were true, she couldn't trust Jack's answer anyway. "No."

His smile faded a bit. "So, about the room?"

She knew he expected an explanation of some type. Shame she hadn't thought to make one up. "No, you're right. My room is lovely."

"What floor is it on?"

*Damn, damn, damn.* "What's with all the questions? I thought the bridal suite scared you."

The huge stop-your-heart smile returned. "Now, honey, I'm pretty sure I didn't say scared. Men don't admit to those types of things."

"That's very hairy and knuckle-dragging of you."

"My only point was that we might want a change of scenery later. Want to try out a new bed." He tapped the key card against her nose. "Unless, of course, your room is pink. I'm terrified of the color pink."

Her mind finally kicked into gear. Unfortunately, it engaged a half step behind the rest of the conversation. Without thinking, she blurted out the first number that popped into her muddled brain.

"Fifth."

"Fifth?"

"My room." She nodded like a simpleton. He had that effect on her. "Fifth."

"Hmmm."

"Hmmm, what?"

"Nothing." He opened the door but stopped before crossing the threshold.

If he tried to pick her up and carry her across, she'd hit him. The dress was for show only.

"I just figured your room would be on a higher floor," he said.

Just what she needed, a man stuck on replay. "Do you really want to spend the evening talking about the hotel floor plan?"

The corner of his mouth kicked up in that sexy smile again. "No, ma'am."

"Then move it." She stepped in front of him, letting her hips sway a bit for emphasis. The swishing sound of the crinoline stopped her. There was no way he could see her butt under all that white fabric, so why waste the flirty move.

He flipped a switch and bathed the room in a soft white light. Her gaze wandered from the stacks of green and yellow pillows sitting on the streamlined beige sofa to the classic cherry furniture. Not her style. Too tidy and perfect, but he fit in here.

The floor-to-ceiling windows in the airy sitting room opened to the bright lights of the Strip. A huge canopy bed sat off to her left through the open door. She saw the turned-down sheets and thick inviting comforter.

He could throw a wild bash and she'd never even know.

Funny how the alleged party boy's room didn't show any evidence of any actual partying. Good thing she had those sleeping pills in her purse. One slipped into his drink and she'd have the time she needed to search the room and get the hell out of there.

She felt an unexpected pang of regret at the idea of leaving him. The idea of hanging around, spending a few hours seeing how Jack's charm translated in bed, tempted her.

"Let's help you out of this." He didn't wait for an invitation. He slid her zipper down before she could stop him.

"Whoa, sailor!" She grabbed for the front of the dress as the back fell away.

"What's wrong?"

"Aren't you a fast worker?"

His hands stilled. "Believe it or not, that's not flattering to a guy."

Great, now she'd offended all of that testosterone bottled up inside those pants. She turned in his arms and concentrated very hard on not enjoying the brush of his fingers against her bare skin. Or, the heat that speared through her stomach when she looked into those eyes.

"So, the words quick, speedy—"

"All bad," he said.

"Good to know."

"But, I'm willing to slow down if it means I can linger over your soft skin for an hour or two." He nibbled on her shoulder, then soothed the spot with a line of tiny kisses. His mouth sparked life into her nerve endings as his palms stroked her shoulders.

She wasn't there for kissing. She was . . . Why the hell wasn't he kissing her?

As if he read her mind, he lifted his head and stared down at her. "Better speed?"

Damn near perfect. "Yeah."

"I aim to please."

Then he lowered his mouth in a long, groaning kiss. Lips moved over hers, bold and daring, caressing and hard. There was nothing hesitant or unsure in his touch. He staked a claim with his mouth and hands, robbing her senses of any control or common sense.

When his tongue slipped inside her mouth, sliding against her teeth before dipping deep, she was lost. Her body locked against his from breast to thigh. Every inch of him molded to her.

She instinctively snuggled his impressive erection between her legs, despite the yards of material separating them. Her hands wandered across his broad shoulders and down to rest on his trim waist. The tour confirmed what she already knew. The body he hid under all that professional clothing was angular and firm and muscled. Perfect.

He broke off the kiss and rested his forehead against hers. "Damn."

Uh-huh. What he said.

Before she could protest and order him back to the kissing, he inched away, letting a breath of air seep between their bodies. Then he swept the dress off her shoulders, down to her waist, then to the floor.

And stopped cold. "What the hell?"

The underwear. She forgot all about her choice of undergarments this morning. A real bride would wear something skimpy and see-through. Probably something daring and a bit over-the-top. Maybe a pair of thigh-highs with those lacy bands. Not a light blue underwire cotton bra with matching blue-and-green-striped boxer briefs.

In her role, her underwear should scream, "Take me now." Hers shouted, "Let's get Chinese food." Functional but not sexy. Not bridal.

She decided to play dumb. "Not a fan of sporty?"

"Oh, they work for me." His gaze traveled down her legs

and back to her face again, burning every inch of her as he went. "Just a surprise, that's all. But, then, you're full of surprises."

If he wanted a surprise, he'd get one in a minute or two. One of the "ewww" variety. She tried to remember if she shaved her legs today. Or yesterday. Or even that week.

The original plan was to get him a hooker then work from behind the scenes to get the information she needed. No shaving required for stakeout work. But the plan had changed, and now she filled in the role of bait. Not that she was complaining.

"I'm a practical gal."

"With killer legs." He skimmed his fingertips over the tops of her breasts where they plumped out over her bra. "Baby-soft skin and brightest green eyes I've ever seen."

"You keep talking like that and, well, you just keep talking like that." And touching her. He should absolutely keep touching her.

"I need a second."

She dropped her hand below his waist and cupped the impressive bulge in his pants. A gentle squeeze wiped out any doubt about what she already felt against her belly. "Oh, I don't think so. You seem ready, willing and able to me."

He moaned and pressed a hard kiss against her lips. "I'll be right back."

"Gotta tell ya, Jack, your timing needs some work." It was perfect, actually, but she decided to tweak him a bit for fun.

"This will teach me to drink when I have a pretty lady on my arm."

Funny, she didn't remember seeing him finish even one glass all evening. "Who am I to stop Mother Nature? I'll be right here when you get back."

"Feel free to try the bed. You rolling around naked in my silk sheets, now that's a picture I've been waiting to see." He winked, then disappeared into the bathroom.

Naked and sheets weren't going to happen no matter how much that particular fantasy danced in her head. Damn, that man could kiss. And caress. And smile. And, well, a whole bunch of naughty things.

She waited less than a second, then slipped off her uncomfortable shoes and started snooping. His briefcase and laptop sat in the bedroom. She decided to take on one room at a time and riffled through the manila folders on the coffee table first. Nothing there but unsigned contracts and some business financial statements.

She knew she should move on, but she peeked at the documents anyway. She started flipping pages. Then her progress slowed. They were very well done financial statements. She skimmed her finger down the columns and admired the professional work. The kind of work she used to do back when she did that kind of thing. Now she did the informal investigator thing. For today, anyway.

If she could find the right folder, she could get out of there. But she couldn't leave yet. Not when she owed Mark.

God knew she needed to find a real job and get back to work. With six hundred dollars in her checking account and the condo mortgage due in two weeks, she hovered around desperation level. In four short months, she'd lost her job, blown her career, run out of options and pushed a good man like Mark Rudolph right to the edge. Fixing everything else in her life could wait until she fixed this part with Mark.

Unless she blew that, too.

Anyone who knew her knew she wasn't qualified to snoop around for evidence. She hardly qualified as the covert spy type. Couldn't even lie about the free cable in her condo. Turned herself in and paid the fine. As an overeducated but out-of-work accountant and beginner financial planner, her only credential for this snooping project she'd assigned herself was an interest in mysteries and true crime.

It helped that all of a sudden Jack possessed the self-restraint of a teenage boy holding his first condom. Thanks to his cool, deep voice, so did she. Shoulders the width of a doorway and a face women would mud wrestle over didn't hurt either.

She'd seen his photo before she flew to Las Vegas to find him. He was a public figure back in San Diego. The kind of guy with his name on both the business page and the society page of the paper. A few hours on the Internet and she knew all about Jack's playboy past, his tendency to engage in month-long flings with beautiful but boring women, his habit of working more hours than actually existed in a day and his love of the mixed drink.

But, damn, nothing had prepared her for the live version of Jack MacAllister. For the full force of his charm when he turned it on high. Apparently, he didn't have a low.

Yeah, no reporter had picked up on that helpful piece of information. That would have been good to know before she started down this road and her clothes hit the floor.

She heard the water running and threw down the files. Time flipped by and there she stood. Empty-handed.

Not anymore. Time to get to work. She reached for the champagne. The cork flew across the room with an unexpected pop before landing in a thud against the sofa pillows. Bubbly liquid raced over her hand as she grabbed up two glasses.

She had only a few seconds to dump her pill mixture in his drink, which would send Jack drifting into a deep sleep. Then she could search through his private property in peace. Of course, she needed to find the damn pills first.

She fumbled through her fancy purse, every second cursing her previous decision to dump the contents of her huge shoulder bag into the tiny dressier one.

*Where. Are. They. Where are they? Wherearethey?*

With one eye focused on the bathroom door and the other on the dark silk lining, she searched. Her fingers closed on a bottle. She yanked too hard and pulled too fast. The container bounced off her palm and rolled under the coffee table, but not before winging through the air and sending small white pills bouncing all over the carpet.

"Damn it." She'd spent the last five years of her life handling complex tax returns for huge companies and assisting in investment strategies. Now she couldn't open a plastic bottle without making a hash of it.

Thanks to the thick pile, the pills stayed where they landed. She grabbed up one and plopped it into the golden liquid. Then she dropped to her knees, butt hanging in the air, and tried to collect the rest of the damning evidence. She figured she had two seconds before Jack walked back in the room and caught her crawling around the floor. Not the easiest position to explain so she decided not to get caught at all.

# Chapter Three

What the hell was she doing on the floor? Women usually waited for him to join them before crawling around on the carpet. Not Laine. No, she had her own way of doing everything.

Jack closed the bathroom door without so much as a click. He'd seen enough. What he'd seen, he had no idea. Snooping? Testing the carpet fibers? He had no idea. He'd gone into the bathroom to conduct some spying of his own. Laine's dumped-bride story didn't fit with anything else about her. He wanted to know why.

He wanted to be wrong because he just plain *wanted* her. Turned out his skepticism made sense. Everyone said he was paranoid. That he had issues with trust. Right. Maybe he had problems trusting because so few people acted as if they deserved any.

Looked like Laine was just one more person with an angle. He was immune to it now. He actually expected it. He just couldn't figure out exactly what he got wrong about Laine or how far she would go, straight to bed or stop before.

Since his dick didn't care about her nosiness or her motives, he was willing to test for her breaking point. After all, if she wanted to use him, he may as well use her back. But, damn, what was the world coming to when a man couldn't trust a woman in a wedding dress?

He'd spent weeks trying to figure out how to deal with his business partner and former best friend. Breaking through to Mark and finding their company's missing money occupied most of his thoughts lately. Now he had to figure out how to deal with Laine. A guy couldn't catch a break.

He threw open the door to be greeted by nothing but a fine ass encased in the cutest little feminine briefs he'd ever seen. "Laine?"

She squealed and jerked, banging her head off the underside of the glass-top coffee table. "Ouch!"

He rushed over and helped her to her feet. "What are you doing?"

"Trying out a self-inflicted lobotomy." She rubbed her head and winced at the contact.

"How'd that work for you?"

"Not so great."

"I probably could have told you that and saved you the trouble."

"Yeah, well, your timing stinks."

"At least you didn't pass out." With his luck, a concussion remained a possibility. He gently massaged her skull. No bumps. Pupils appeared normal. Eyeballs firmly in her head. All good signs.

"Do you need a hospital?"

"No," she mumbled under her breath. "I'm only seeing one of you."

He wrapped an arm around her shoulders and eased her onto the couch. "Think how much fun two of me would be."

She snorted.

"So, you always crawl around on the floor in hotel rooms?"

"Only when I drop something," she mumbled against his shoulder.

Uh-huh. Like a good excuse for her questionable behavior. "What did you lose?"

"Uh, my, umm . . . my purse."

He glanced at the upended bag, with its insides spilled all over its outside. "You mean the one sitting upside down on top of the table."

"Uh."

"The same one not on the floor," he said.

She followed his gaze, and her hand stilled in her hair. "I picked it up and put it there right before you came in."

"And decided to hang out under the table for fun?" Yeah, that made sense. About as much as everything else she'd told him.

"I live for pain."

He raised an eyebrow but didn't comment.

"I didn't mean it that way," she rushed to explain.

"Okay."

"No, really—"

"Laine, I get it."

Her hand moved to that fleshy part of her chest right above her bra. He loved that part of her. Her creamy skin caught him in a trance.

"You scared me to death," she said.

"You look good to me. Good enough to eat." Pretty damn good for a liar.

"You hungry?"

Was she kidding? "Not even a little."

"Oh."

"I thought you'd try the bed while I was gone." He hesitated to see if she'd rise to the bait. She didn't. "Not the coffee table."

"I was on my way."

"And?"

She didn't answer but stood up, walked to the windows and stared out at the lights on the Strip. He sensed she needed some space. Probably wanted to concoct a new story without him watching too closely. Worked for him because from this angle he could admire her ass without having to keep one hand on his wallet.

She wasn't tall, maybe five-foot-five, but her legs were long and lean. Her tight ass and firm thighs spoke to a commitment to exercise or the luck of good genes. She was small and curvy, every inch of her sleek and sexy. The tiny boxer briefs made the blood in his erection pound.

Whatever snooping-related thing she was doing, she wasn't very good at it. The computer printouts stuck out of his folders at all angles. He squinted down at the floor. White pills blazed a trail from inside her purse and across the carpet. What in the hell was that about?

He left for the bathroom for ten seconds and she managed to throw his stuff all over the room and, and . . . what? He couldn't explain the pills no matter how many ways he tried.

A puzzle. Nothing about her fit. A smart guy would kick her out or run for cover. Not him. Despite everything else he knew about her, which was nothing, he burned with the need to touch her. To bury himself deep inside her until she moaned and begged for more.

He even wanted to sit around and talk with her some more. And what the hell was that about?

That was the movie version playing in his head, but he knew the evening wasn't going to end that way. He picked up a pill and touched it to his tongue. Acidic. Aspirin? Maybe there was a reasonable explanation, like snooping through a stranger's personal items gave her a headache.

Time to up the ante. "I see you poured some champagne."

She turned around and treated him to a megawatt smile.

One that fell as soon as she saw him holding the glass. "Uh, yeah."

The "uh" thing returned. Interesting. "Come here and we'll toast our night together."

"I'm not a big drinker." She said the words so fast they ran together into one big slur.

"I saw you down a few beers earlier."

"I meant champagne."

Sure. That was the problem. "Since you went to the trouble of pouring, let's indulge. No need to waste the casino's finest."

She walked so slowly he was surprised she didn't move backward. After what felt like an hour, she reached him and for a glass. With her fingers touching the glass in the same excited way she would hold a petri dish filled with an infectious disease, she took a baby sip. The liquid barely touched her tongue before she lowered the glass again.

"Problem?" he asked, his voice deep and comforting.

"Uh, no." This time she gulped down another swallow and a good bit of air. The resulting coughing fit nearly bounced her breasts right out of her little bra.

"You okay?" He guessed the only problem was with whatever dumb plan she'd cooked up for him, and her desire to stay sober for it. He eased the glass from her fingers and set it on the table.

She came up for a breath. "Aren't you having any?"

"I'm not drinking. You're intoxicating enough." Another lame line, but he didn't care. They were playing a game. She just hadn't clued him in on the rules yet.

"You're not—"

"Why don't I show you the view from the bedroom?"

Those grass green eyes widened. "Uh . . ."

"Unless you prefer the couch?" He leaned down and kissed her. The sweet taste of champagne played on her soft lips.

At first she just stood there, still and cool. Then her palms slid up his chest. She massaged his neck, rasping her fingernails against the sensitive dip at the top of his shoulders.

It was all the invitation he needed. Her touch set him on fire. He filled his hands with that perfect tight ass and squeezed her lower body against his. Frantic drugging kisses passed between them until soft mewing sounds rumbled up the back of her throat.

Damn, he wanted her.

"Jack?"

"Yeah, honey."

"We need a bed."

# Chapter Four

She was all over him. As intoxicating as the finest wine and as invigorating as a heavy dose of Viagra.

Laine, or whatever the hell her name really was, appeared wide awake. Not sleepy. Not doped up. She hadn't so much as yawned.

*Thank God.*

Her hands tore at his clothing, untucking his shirt and reaching for the buttons. She rained kisses in a trail across his chin until she arrived at his waiting mouth. Then she didn't hesitate. Her lips closed over his in a kiss full of promise. Of need.

Bare skin slid against him. Everywhere he was hard, she was soft and smooth. Her skin smelled like roses, feminine and sweet, tempting him to lose his mind in her. With his nose buried in her silky hair, he inhaled, dragging her sweet scent deep into his lungs.

Her fingers tangled in his shirt opening. Rather than perform a slow striptease, she ripped open the seam and sent the white buttons flying. Between searing kisses, he watched her stroke her fingernails across his exposed chest. Felt the tiny bites against his flesh.

"Seems only fair you strip down." Her tongue licked across his lips. "Underwear to underwear."

"Skin to skin."

She nibbled on his ear. "Body in body."

Damn, if this was a game, he was in and ready to play. "Absolutely."

He tried to return to the kissing part of the program, but she stopped him. "I thought we were headed for the bedroom. Unless you want to try the coffee table."

"What makes you think I can move?" Hell, since all of his blood rushed to his lower half, he couldn't even see.

"You were doing fine a few seconds ago," she said in a voice sultry enough to melt his kneecaps.

"Until tripping over the ottoman became a very real possibility. Doesn't seem very debonair of me to fall down at your feet."

"Oh, I don't know about that. The idea of you sitting at my feet has its merits."

He took one more step until the edge of the sofa table rammed into the back of his upper thigh. "Damn it!"

"Very smooth."

His leg throbbed. "You won't think it's funny if I've lost feeling below the waist."

"Well, let's see." She brushed her hand over the front of his pants, back and forth until he strained against her fingertips. "Everything appears to be in working order."

A moan worked its way up his throat. "You have the magic touch."

"We should get those pants off so I can look at your injury."

Who was he to argue? He pressed her back against the bedroom doorway and trapped her wrists against her sides. Holding her there, watching her chest rise and fall from the force of her heavy breathing. Her flushed cheeks and puffed wet lips told him what he needed to know. She wanted him. Despite everything else, she wanted him.

His need for her clawed at his insides until he couldn't breathe. "I can't wait," he whispered.

"Take me." She gave her order through deep, branding kisses.

Energy flowed through him. Every sense clicked to high alert. Liar or not, he had to have her. He'd figure out her secrets later. Let her apologize, then go again.

"Bed." That was the only word his mind could form.

She eased out of his arms. With a slow, sure walk she headed into the bedroom, her fingertips touching his, keeping the slight bond between them. She looked back over her shoulder, her smoky gaze daring him to follow.

When she sat on the edge of the bed with her bare feet set wide apart, he forgot all about her searching and lying. All about the pills and the dress. She was a sensual, feeling woman. One in control of her sexuality and comfortable with it. No hiding. No stupid insecurities. Just desire.

He stepped into the space between her soft thighs and raked his fingers through her hair. Each strand, silky and smooth, fell against his hand. "You are so beautiful."

"So are you." She gazed up at him as her hand stroked his erection through his pants. "So strong."

"God, Laine, touch me."

"Like this?" She leaned in and pressed a kiss against the cloth, making his dick jump in response.

"Any way is fine so long as you don't stop."

"Or, like this?" Slow and easy, one tick at a time, she pulled down his zipper and freed him. She closed her palm over him and squeezed.

"Damn." The word hissed out between clenched teeth.

"Harder?" She pressed a kiss against his lower abdomen as her hand glided up and down in a sure, steady rhythm.

This time he moaned, unable to focus on anything other than the feel of her soft hand as she smoothed over him. "Laine."

"Tell me what you want, Jack."

"You." He'd never meant it more in his life.

"That's it?"

"Only you."

"Let me help." She slid her hands under the waistband of his briefs and pulled the gray cotton down and off until he stood before her in nothing but an open shirt.

"Your turn," he said.

She told him he was beautiful, and the compliment wasn't a lie. Other things, yes. Not that.

His body fell in a deep V from his shoulders to his waist. Muscles rippled across his chest. Tall for her at six foot, but still perfect. Not fat. No marks. Just smooth, tanned skin.

She pumped her hand up and down his shaft and watched as his eyes slipped shut in response. He was long and thick as he pulsed against her. With every squeeze, she could hear his breathing grow more shallow. See his arms tense each time she tightened her fingers.

Professionalism and common sense be damned. She wanted this for her. Nothing had been for her in the four months since the regulators shut down her office and left her reputation in tatters, despite her innocence.

She had thought that was the worst moment of her life until Mark walked in. He wanted to know where the money he entrusted to her had gone. She didn't know. She didn't know where any of her clients' money had gone. The underhanded dealings happening in her office were news to her.

Mark vented his anger on her. Then fell apart in front of her eyes as he told her all about his partner Jack and the financial problems back at the office. Problems Mark blamed on Jack and used as an excuse to set up that secret business account.

Laine understood. All the disappointment and pain, the frustration and unfairness, that goes with that kind of suspected betrayal. She knew exactly how Mark felt, even though she wondered how he had gotten himself into such a mess. And, if his suspicions about Jack were true.

Nothing she saw about Jack pointed to questionable dealings, but, then, she didn't know him on a business level. She knew him on a very personal level.

She hadn't expected to like him, be comfortable with him or want him. Since she did, she was going to take the opportunity he offered. Somewhere along the line she had stopped being a thinking, feeling woman. That was about to change, too. She wanted Jack, so the rest could wait.

The briefcase would be there a few hours from now. She had some time left before she had to morph from fake bride back to unemployed accountant. She planned to enjoy every minute in between.

She scooted back on the bed, and his eyes shot open. "Damn, Laine, don't stop."

"I thought we'd try some of that advanced stuff you promised."

"Only if you're ready to lose the underwear."

The challenge had been issued. She wasn't about to back down now. Not when she needed this so much. Reaching behind her, she flicked open her bra clasp. While one hand held the flimsy piece of cotton to her breasts, the other peeled the straps off her shoulders.

"Drop it." His deep voice boomed in the quiet room.

"Is that an order?"

"It can be anything you want so long as you lose the top."

His words rocketed through her. Her insides melted as her limbs grew heavy and her heart kicked into gear. Everything about him spoke to that feminine core hidden deep inside her.

A flash of guilt hit her. She should walk out. Stop the lie and get out before Jack realized why she was really there and ruined the moment. She dropped her hands, exposing her bare breasts instead.

"Beautiful," he whispered, his warm gaze never leaving her flushed skin.

The decision made, she lay back on the down comforter with her knees raised and her arms flung high over her head. The position made her vulnerable, and for some reason, that didn't scare her.

She didn't want mere sex. She wanted to be taken. To lose control. To lose herself in another person, in him, if only for a few hours. To be all those things a serious accountant usually wasn't but that a female spy could be.

She repeated her previous command. "Now, Jack."

His slow, sexy smile returned. "Yes, ma'am. Anything to please."

He placed one knee on the bed, then the other. Starting with her right calf, he kissed a trail of white-hot kisses up her leg to her knee; then he went back and treated her left leg to the same. When he eased his broad shoulders between her thighs and smoothed his palms across her skin to the edge of her briefs, her hips flexed off the mattress.

"Jack—"

"Shhh. Relax and enjoy."

He tunneled his fingers under the cotton bands around her legs until his thumbs reached the center of her. "Damn, baby, you're soaking wet."

"Please."

He swept his thumbs across her, one after the other, in a steady beat that set her blood thrumming through her lower body. With each pass her hips bounced, grinding against his hands. Her internal muscles clenched, and her shoulders pressed deep into the covers.

"God, yes." The harsh whisper escaped her before she could stop it.

"That's it, baby. Come for me." Fingers pressed deep inside of her while his thumb moved in lazy circles over her swollen clit.

"Jack." She grabbed fists full of comforter on either side of her body. "Now."

He stopped.

"Jack!" Her head whipped forward. "What are you doing?"

"I have to taste you." He scrambled to his knees and slid his hands under her. With a hard tug, he dragged the briefs down her legs and threw them on the floor.

He spread her thighs wide and stared at her most private place. Her body was open to him. There was nothing standing between them.

"Jack?"

"That's better."

He threw something, and it landed next to her right arm. "What are—"

Whatever she was going to say flew right out of her head when his mouth closed over her. His hot tongue plunged deep inside, followed by a finger, then another. He caressed and sucked, kissed and licked, until her body bucked and her head fell back in surrender.

The orgasm crashed through her on a scream. She chanted his name as her body trembled and rocked. When the last wave left her, he rested his forehead against her inner thigh.

"As I said, beautiful." He kissed the soft skin next to his mouth. "Amazing."

"You were pretty incredible yourself." Damn, she couldn't stop panting. Choppy breathing echoed in her ears.

Sure she'd had a decent roll or two between the sheets in her twenty-seven years of life. This wasn't her first time, or even her first good time. But giving her body over to pleasure, letting herself go and enjoying the moment knowing this was all she could ever have—that was a first.

And, if someone could be considered a tongue expert, Jack was it.

"You're not going to sleep on me, are you?" His voice rumbled against her thigh.

"I'm kind of hoping we're not done."

He chuckled, the sound so rich and carefree, she had to join him. "I'm thinking I've only gotten started."

"Good man."

He moved up her limp body and balanced his weight on his elbows. With his erection lodged against her opening, he dipped down and captured her mouth in a slow, mind-blowing kiss. Her lips tingled as she waited for him to slip deep inside her.

"Jack, I need—"

"Me, too." He grabbed up a foil packet and ripped it open with his teeth.

Now she knew what he'd thrown on the bed.

"Laine?"

With his hands behind her knees, he pressed her legs back and toward her chest, exposing her to his gaze and body. From this position he would fill her completely. She would be totally at his mercy, vulnerable to his movements. She would feel every drive.

"Laine?" His voice was louder this time, more insistent.

His erection nudged against her, but he didn't press inside. Desire pulsed off of him, but still he waited, as if needing permission to enter her.

"Yes. Jack, yes."

He didn't hesitate. Inch by inch he pushed inside her, not stopping but going slow enough to give her time to adjust to his size, to the sensual feel of his body gliding into hers. Then he moved, in and out, each time filling her completely before retreating. The friction stole her breath, made every inch of her body flash to life.

His fingers folded into hers and held her arms beside her head. He rested his cheek against hers. "Baby, I can't hold back."

"Don't." She tightened her palms against his. "Come for me."

His movements lost all control, became more erratic. His chest heaved as her body lifted off the mattress to meet each thrust. When she clenched her thighs against his waist, the speed increased again. The shivers rippling inside her grew more intense until they exploded and washed over her.

Her climax touched off his. She squeezed her legs one last time and pressed her hands against his lower back, bringing his body impossibly tight against hers. Tension rolled off his shoulders, and with one last push, he stiffened, then fell on top of her with a groan.

They lay there quiet and unmoving. After a few seconds he pushed back up on his arms and stared down at her. After their intimacy, she should have felt confident. Not embarrassed or vulnerable. So, why the sudden wave of insecurity?

"Hi there," he said.

She traced her finger over his swollen lips. "Hi."

He grabbed her hand and kissed her fingers. "You're amazing."

Confidence seeped back into her consciousness. "You're not too bad yourself."

"Gee, ma'am, that's sweet."

"I'm thinking you've done this once or twice."

"I'm hoping to do 'this' once or twice more before morning. After I rest, of course." He rolled to his back and pulled her tight against his side. "I'm not as young as I used to be."

"Now that you're forty-five, you mean."

"Not that age thing again."

She laughed and snuggled down with her head on his shoulder and his arm tight around her. She couldn't help but smile. The man had charm for miles. He was equally impressive between the sheets and outside of them.

She closed her eyes and breathed in his warm, masculine scent. A sense of calm fell over her. Until he opened his stupid mouth and ruined the moment.

"I have to say it."

"What?"

"Your fiancé is an idiot."

Her eyes popped open, all thoughts of relaxing gone. "What?"

"How could that guy let you go?"

She cleared her throat. "You, uh, mean ex fiancé."

"Of course. Ex." He squeezed her in a gentle hug. "What was his name again?"

Damn, what name did she make up for the fake fiancé? "Does it matter?"

"No." He yawned and stretched. "Just wondered."

"Uh-huh."

"Let's rest for a few minutes," he suggested.

Sure, sleeping was going to happen. She listened to his breathing as it changed from rapid to even. She used the time while he drifted off to plan her escape from his bedroom.

Enough fun. She had to get the wedding dress back to its owner. She had to plot her excuse for slipping out in case he caught her in the act. She had to figure out how to search the room without waking him.

She was dead asleep within ten minutes.

# Chapter Five

"This is PMS medicine."

One eyelid popped open at the sound of Jack's stunned voice. Not the most pleasant way to wake up after rounds of incredible lovemaking.

Make that sex. They had sweaty, fun sex. Not lovemaking.

He ranted on. "You tried to poison me with menstrual cramp medicine."

She was barely awake, and he was on a rampage about something. She stared at the top of the canopy bed and tried to put her scrambled thoughts together. She recapped the night in her head. They had sex. Her number one mistake, but it happened and she couldn't take it back.

Didn't want to either. She'd never wanted a man as much as she wanted Jack. Never felt that instant connection before. Then they—

"Do you see this label?" He held a bottle in front of her face, actually smacked it against her nose, then snatched it back and started reading. "For headaches, and bloating. I don't even know what bloating is."

"You're bloated?"

"You're not listening to me."

"Jack, I'm barely awake, and you're talking about headaches."

She tried to put all the pieces together. She lay in a sprawl in Jack's cozy bed. Sure, she'd fallen asleep, but at least she'd had the grace to do that *after*. So, why was he so pissed?

"Woman, what the hell is wrong with you? This crap could make me sterile."

Make him . . . wait. What? "What are you talking about?"

He sat on the edge of the king-sized bed, twirling a pill bottle in his lean hands. "This tell you anything?"

He held the label so close her eyes crossed. But, damn, that could mean only one thing. She'd hoped he hadn't seen the bottle of sleeping pills before running her into the bedroom. Apparently her luck had failed there, too.

How could a good deed go so wrong? She was only trying to help. To fix the mess she—no, make that her bosses—had made. Hell, she was considered an exceptional accountant and up-and-coming financial consultant. No one would hire her now.

"Well, Jack, it tells me you've been busy going through my belongings over the last few hours." She struggled to sound cool when mostly what she felt was disappointment. Their time was about to end.

"I got up a few minutes ago."

"And haven't you been busy during that time?"

"Are you going to explain this?" He pushed that bottle into her face again.

She slapped his hand away. "Only if you clue me in on what's ticking you off."

"Why would you give a guy cramp medicine?"

His complaints finally registered. Did he say cramp medicine? "Cramp—"

"Medicine."

She was never so happy to talk about her periods in her life. "Let me get this straight. You went digging through my purse, found my cramp medicine, as you call it, and decided . . . ?"

"Well, I thought—"

"—that I was trying to turn you into a woman."

"It sounds ridiculous when you say it like that," he mumbled.

"I think that's my point." She pushed her hair off her face.

"I didn't say you wanted me to be a woman."

No, she very much wanted him to continue being a man. "That's something, I guess."

"You were trying to give me meds," he grumbled.

"Why exactly would I do that, Jack?"

A red flush stained his cheeks. "How the hell should I know. This was on the floor."

She grabbed the bottle out of his hand and conducted a quick scan. Not sleeping pills but stuff for her period which had just ended. Man, he was right. She'd dumped the wrong medicine in his champagne. Well, in one of the glasses. He'd grabbed them up so she didn't know which was which.

Further evidence that nothing in her life was running according to plan. "From this, you jumped to the conclusion that I was what?"

He had the grace to look confused. "Trying to put pills in my drink."

Well, he got that part right. "Doesn't that sound a bit strange to you, Jack?"

He massaged the back of his neck. "Yeah, sure. Now it does."

"You're saying there was a point in time in which this cramp medicine scenario didn't sound strange?"

"Gee, Laine, call me suspicious. You said all that crap about money and the cost of my room."

"I'm an accountant." That wasn't exactly a lie.

"An . . . did you say accountant?"

"I do financial work for individuals and businesses. Help with investments and tax issues."

"Oh."

"Yeah. Oh. I commented on your extravagant spending because I count money for a living."

His mouth hung open. "Shit."

"Uh-huh."

"I thought—"

"You thought what?" She decided to go with the righteous indignation angle. It certainly looked better than the truth in this instance.

"Nothing."

She sat up and swung her legs over the side of the bed. Seemed like the perfect time for a dramatic exit. She blocked out how much she hated the idea of leaving him and focused on her work and getting that dress back on time. If she could lure him into the other room, then take a few minutes to search through his stuff, she could get out of the hotel. Hell, out of Vegas.

Without warning the lights blinked out, plunging the room into complete darkness. She flicked the switches next to the bed, but the lights stayed off, and the heavy automatic drapes didn't move.

She froze. "Jack?"

"What the hell is happening now?"

Nothing, as far as she could tell. Not a sound. Even the air stood still.

"What's going on?" She could hear him moving around but couldn't see a shadow.

"Power loss, I guess. Probably related to the construction."

"You said that was another building." She heard shuffling, then a sharp crack.

"Damn it!"

"What?"

"Found the dresser." He let out an impressive stream of profanity.

"With what exactly?"

"My leg."

"Same one you injured earlier?"

He ignored the question. "There's nothing on out here either. Must have blown a transformer."

Enough of this. She stood up but stayed low, her body hugging the bed and her fingers skimming along the top for guidance. "Maybe it's a fire."

"We'd know," he said.

"How?"

"By the flames, smoke, fire. I don't know, sirens." He grunted and grumbled. "Any one of those things would be a giveaway."

"You don't have to be rude."

"Yeah, well, my leg hurts."

"Big baby," she mumbled.

"Easy to tell you're not a nurse," he shouted back.

"Is it bleeding?"

"I can't exactly see to tell." He sounded far away and as foul as could be.

"Where are you?"

"Living room."

"Throw back the drapes."

She navigated her way around the bedroom furniture and into the other room. Jack held the thick curtain and stared out at the Strip. The lights from the street and casino billboards lit up most of the room.

He stood naked and proud. From this angle she could

admire his firm butt at her leisure with the feel of those strong shoulders and that muscled body fresh in her mind.

She moved up beside him and stared out at the flickering lights of the casino across the street. Despite the early morning hour just before three, people milled around, and cars packed the road.

"It looks as if everyone in Vegas has power but us." His attention focused on what was going on outside.

Her attention centered on him.

She pressed her hands against the cool glass but turned her head to study his perfect profile. The straight nose and firm chin. "Think it will come on soon?"

"Sure. The casino will lose a fortune if everything isn't back up and running in a few minutes."

His penis lay against his thigh. Even soft, his size commanded attention. "Spoken like a true businessman."

"Yeah, well, can you imagine what the casino must look like. Those people, lights out and all that money on the tables. Damn, I'm sure Alex is going nuts as we speak."

"Most people are probably gone or in their rooms by now."

He looked at her and smiled. "You don't know much about Vegas, do you?"

She searched through her mental file of lies. Had she told him she knew anything about Las Vegas? She knew all about San Diego, but that wasn't the question.

Since she couldn't remember, she went with the safe answer. "Why?"

"This city doesn't sleep. My guess is that people are acting like idiots down there."

"Good thing we're up here." Where she could wrestle him back to bed and enjoy another round of lovemaking.

Maybe figure out a way to make their time together last a bit longer. "And, you're right. Alex and the rest of the management people are probably all over the maintenance staff right now trying to get the power back up."

"I hope," he said, distracted by the situation.

"Not me."

He balanced his shoulder against the window and frowned at her. "Care to fill me in?"

"How 'bout I show you instead?"

His eyes narrowed, but he didn't move. "I'm game."

"I need you ready, not game." She leaned in and kissed him full on the mouth. When he started to put his arms around her, she ducked out of his embrace.

"I like this so far."

"Will you do something for me?"

"Sure."

"Face the glass."

"Laine, I don't think—"

"Hands on the window. Feet apart." She raised an eyebrow, daring him to argue.

With a slow, jerky move, he turned around and obeyed her request. "Now what?"

She pressed her breasts against his back and reached around to place her palms against his bare chest. As her hands caressed his muscles, she kissed every inch across the top of his shoulders.

"Will you let me be in charge, Jack?"

"Damn, you feel so good against me." He lifted his hands off the glass.

"Nope. Hands back down. No touching."

"Laine."

"This is my show." She trailed her fingers down his chest and circled his penis.

"Oh, man."

"Who needs lights?" she whispered in his ear, licking her tongue around the ridge. "We can feel our way."

"You're killing me."

"Seducing you."

His erection grew, filling her hand. His body warmed against hers, his skin damp and hot to the touch. He leaned down until his forehead touched the window. "I'm not going to make it."

She rubbed one palm up and down on his thigh while her other hand pumped up and down on his penis. "I need you ready."

"I'm ready, hon." At his sharp intake of breath, she moved her hand faster.

"I'll be the judge of that."

"Can't get much bigger."

"Pessimist. Let's try."

Her hands wandered over his body, enjoying the hardness of his muscles as she took in the musky scent of his skin. When his knees buckled, she kept up her gentle torture.

"I have to sit down." His chest shook from the force of his breathing.

"Perfect."

He lifted his head and turned around, capturing her mouth in a kiss. When he broke contact, they were both short of breath.

"I can't last much longer."

She kissed him again. "You don't have to."

"Where?"

"Chair."

They barely made it.

He wrapped his arms around her waist and carried her to the overstuffed chair. "Are you—"

"Shhh." She pushed him back until he fell into the seat.

She braced her knees around his hips and slowly lowered her mouth to his ear. "How many condoms do we have?"

"Not enough."

"Then we'll have to make each one last."

# Chapter Six

Jack tried the front door for a second time. Damn thing still didn't budge. The situation hadn't turned desperate, but it would soon. The air had turned warm and stale a few hours after they got locked in together. Breathing in weighed on his chest. In a few more hours warm air would change to hot, and he'd be ready to claw his way through the window.

He adjusted the heavy curtains across the back of the desk chair to let light into the living room before walking into the other room and back to bed. Without electricity, and since he had no idea where he put his watch, he relied on his internal alarm clock. Still morning, probably around six.

He slipped into bed next to Laine and threw the covers down until they covered only their legs. Her skin felt hot and damp when he wrapped an arm around her shoulders and pulled her tight against his side. The closeness, the touch of skin to bare skin, felt so right. So natural despite the heat.

He couldn't remember a time when having a woman cozy up next to him gave him a sense of peace. Over the years, the women who had joined him between the sheets had known the score. Good sex and short-term companionship followed by an amicable ending.

With Laine he didn't want neat and tidy. Didn't want to think about goodbye. Something about her spoke to something in him, and he wanted to take it apart and examine it.

A tiny gurgle escaped her lips, but her eyes didn't so much as flicker. Instead, her body slid against his as if they'd spent a lifetime sleeping together.

*Perfect*. He needed her defenses down for their chat. He guessed with her financial background, she was following him around looking for a new financial client. The pieces didn't really fit since Laine didn't strike him as being that single-minded and heartless, but at least he had a theory he could work with.

He just needed her to fess up so that he could politely turn down a professional relationship with her and focus on their bedroom relationship.

After all the lovemaking, all that friction, she hadn't opened up and told him the truth. Or anything. He knew how and where she liked his fingers to move across her flesh. The amount of pressure needed to force her heels into the mattress as her back arched toward the ceiling. How much licking and sucking she could tolerate before she came.

He knew all that and nothing else. Even her last name remained a mystery. If they had any hope of moving past the lies standing between them, he needed her to open up. Trust. It was all about trust. In less than twenty-four hours, she had wormed her way into his head.

What she did for him in bed, the way her breasts filled his palms and her body grew wet and dewy from the slightest contact, bordered on indescribable. He didn't know what he felt for Laine, but letting her go before he figured it all out wasn't an option.

"You awake?" He whispered the question when he wanted to shout.

She dug her nose deeper into his side. "Arghpf."

"I'm pretty sure that's not a word."

"Grarf."

"Or that."

"Yeff," she mumbled against his skin.

"Still sleepy?"

"When did we sleep?" Her words still slurred together, but at least they made some sense.

"There were ten minutes in there somewhere when you stopped climbing all over me."

The sleepiness didn't lessen her quickness. "You wish," she mumbled.

Yes, he did.

She stretched her arms above her head before settling them back on his chest. "It's hot in here."

"Lack of air-conditioning will do that."

"It's kind of sexy now," she said. "You know, all steamy and forbidden, but it will be gross soon."

"We have some time before the heat fully descends and we suffocate."

"That's a lovely visual image."

"I aim to please."

"And you do."

He heard the smile in her voice. "Stop. You'll make me blush."

"I doubt that's possible."

Time to get some questions answered. "So, where did you say you were from?"

Her body morphed from near liquid to granite in one second. Every inch of her went still. "What?"

Amazing how her enunciation cleared right up and the sleepiness wiped away. "I asked where you live."

"Uh, why?"

He noticed her "uh" thing returned right on schedule. "Seems like a logical question under the circumstances."

She dragged her fingernails in small circles on his bare stomach. "Those would be?"

"Well, there's the fact I've seen you naked, for one. Then there's the being inside you for four hours thing."

"I get it."

He laughed. "There's a joke in that statement somewhere."

For a second, her fingernails dug into his chest. "I thought we were going to keep this light."

"I figured we passed that point three orgasms ago." This time he felt the sting of her fingers.

"Fine. Southern California."

He could almost hear her teeth grind together. "Excuse me?"

"I said, Southern California."

"Ahh." He rested his palm over hers. It was either that or let her dig a hole through to his internal organs. "Any particular part of the state, or do you actually live in the entire southern region?"

She sat up and pulled the silk sheet over her body and up to her chin. With her mussed blond hair and pink skin, she looked like the poster child for debauchery.

How did he ever limit her looks to cute. That description didn't cover half of it. She qualified as the hottest woman he'd ever seen. They'd burned up the sheets. Compatible in their likes and needs.

He wanted her. Liked the way she challenged him. He just wished he could trust her.

"What's going on, Jack?"

He folded his arms behind his head and stared up at her with as innocent a look as he could muster. "Meaning?"

"You made the rules. All that stuff about no last names—"

"MacAllister."

Her mouth opened and shut two times before she continued. "I suppose that's your name."

She wasn't very quick in the morning. "I'm not sure what else it could be," he said.

"I didn't ask."

"I know that."

She twisted the sheet until she nearly shredded it in her hands. "We agreed to no strings."

"Asking where you live is a string?"

"Of course."

She was unraveling by the minute. He wondered what would happen when he asked her an important question. "Let's try this. If I ask your shoe size, would you be offended?"

"I'd think you're either nuts or you've been hitting the champagne without me."

Funny how she could run so hard and so fast without ever moving an inch. "Your shoe size is more intimate than your zip code."

"Seven. Happy?"

He actually was. Another laugh rumbled up his chest, and he didn't try to stop it. "Score one for you."

She clutched the soft sheet even harder to her breasts. "Is my dress size next?"

"How about this one." He sat up and leaned against the headboard so he could pull her back down with him when the opportunity arose. "Are you really an accountant?"

She frowned at him. "Would I make up something like that? If I were lying, I'd say astronaut or something equally exciting."

"Who knows what a woman from all of Southern California might do?"

"Go ahead. Quiz me on any part of the tax code. I'm ready."

"The abridged version was more my thing."

The tension left her body. "I happen to know it backward and forward. Can even give you tips. Suggest investment strategies. Tell you how to shelter income."

"Fascinating stuff."

"Anything you want to know. Just ask."

"I'll pass."

She finally cracked a smile. "Don't whine to me later if you want tax information. You had your chance for a lesson."

Something about her smile made him forget her sins. "Story of my life."

"What about you?"

He played dumb. "Me?"

She kneeled in front of him. Her hand maintained the death grip on the sheet, but the rest of her body relaxed. "You're so big on show-and-tell all of a sudden. Spill it. Tell me all about you."

She'd boxed him right into that corner. Spooky woman. Telling her part of the truth couldn't hurt anything. Her reaction might even give him some clue about her intentions.

He settled a hand on her upper thigh. He could feel the heat radiating off of her through the sheet. "There's no big secret. I'm a businessman from San Diego and here for a little relaxation."

"I notice you didn't say vacation."

"Vacations aren't my thing. The office is never more than a call, fax or e-mail away."

"How exciting for you."

"It's a life." Not much of one since Mark had scammed him, leaving him without anyone to confide in. To trust. "I'm not complaining."

"So, Jack, any particular need for all this sunny relaxation?" She sat there naked and appealing, but her stare bore into him. For some reason, she appeared very interested in his answer.

"Hard time at work. Some problems I'm having trouble resolving."

"Like what?"

End of the show-and-tell. "You're right."

She sat back on her heels. "About what?"

"About this conversation crossing over into forbidden territory."

Her gaze searched his face. A few seconds ticked by before she answered. "Fair enough."

She stepped off the bed, taking the sheet with her in a dramatic sweep. She wrapped the material around her and tucked in the stray ends between her luscious breasts, those same breasts he'd feasted on most of the morning.

"Hey!"

She looked back over her shoulder, her gaze traveling over him like a caress. "You didn't strike me as a guy who minded being naked."

"Only as long as you're tucked in beside me."

"Soon." A sudden sadness shadowed her usually bright green eyes. "Need a break for food."

When she smiled, he smiled back. Everything about her appealed to him. The strength. The smarts. The charm. The body. Her motives were the problem.

"I'd guess you're out of luck on that score. Without electricity, there's no room service. Even the superstar chef they have here can't cook without heat or refrigeration."

"Jack, Jack, Jack." That flirty lilt moved back into her voice. "After all these hours together you still underestimate me."

"Something tells me that would be a mistake."

She dropped the sheet on his feet, revealing inch after inch of creamy skin. Like a trained dog, his dick jumped to attention. When she reached around and grabbed the thick terrycloth robe off the back of the bathroom door, a wave of disappointment flowed through him. She compounded his regret when she covered that mouth-watering body from shoulder to bare feet, with only painted pink toenails visible.

His lower half didn't seem to know the difference. Just

looking at her made him hard. "I certainly don't see a need for clothing of any type. It's too hot in here."

She laughed. "I'll live."

"There's no reason to suffer."

"At least you're consistent. You came up with the clothing-optional thing and insisted on it for most of the evening."

"Do you blame me?"

"No." She leaned down and kissed him. Her lips pressed against his in a painfully sweet move.

He immediately knew something was wrong.

"So, you have a cake in that wedding dress?" he asked.

"Even better. You have a minibar full of food. No need to waste away from hunger when we can recharge and refuel with a stack of nine-dollar candy bars. Sure, you'll need a loan to get out of here, but that's your problem, not mine."

Part of him wanted to believe her, that she really needed food before another round of lovemaking. She conned his lower half into submission. His upper half, the boring and reasonable half, knew better.

"That's not very accountant-like of you, Laine."

"Sometimes my stomach overrules my head."

"Do the people who hand out the CPAs know about this?"

She winked and headed for the door. "You keep my secrets, and I'll keep yours."

Uh-huh. Secrets. Her specialty. "I'll be there in a minute. Save something high in fat and expensive for me."

"Take your time," she called out from the living room.

Right. As if he'd leave her alone.

# Chapter Seven

Laine did the analysis and came to the only conclusion possible. She could be the winner and grand champion in the Dumbest Woman Alive Contest.

Just a few minutes ago she'd lain there safe, even if a little too warm, in Jack's arms, fantasizing about seeing him again after they left Vegas. Then crash. In the aftermath, before their bodies cooled and relaxed, she'd woven stupid daydreams about securing a connection between them.

He'd used the time to think up questions for the grilling to come. Where she lived—where did that come from? Just went to show that passionate lovemaking, witty conversation and a little snuggling didn't always mean something.

Dumb, dumb, dumb.

Well, the stupid-woman show was over. She swallowed back a lump of regret and tried to figure out how she could miss Jack when she hadn't even left his room. She feared the loss would stay with her. Finding a smart, attractive, funny man amounted to a miracle these days.

But they shared a one-night stand and nothing more. She played those words over and over again in her mind. Maybe after the third or fourth time she'd believe it.

Rather than wallow in her misfortune, she came up with a new plan. Drop off the dress, go back to her room, do some digging in the briefcase she'd shoved out of Jack's bedroom with her foot while she did that cool sheet trick, then go home and forget about her night with one Jack MacAllister.

Why couldn't he show the side that Mark kept talking about? Jack was either the world's greatest actor or a dual personality. She ran through the litany of wrongs Mark had given her about Jack. Problem was, none of the information Mark had provided matched with her observations over the last few days. Not one thing.

But, she'd figure that out later.

Now she had to run. It was morning, and the real bride would be getting antsy. She'd made a promise to the woman to return the gown. She'd broken enough of those lately. She was determined to keep this one.

Fumbling her way down the dark hotel hallway nearly naked didn't rank as one of the best ideas of the century. The other options didn't look so great either. Jack had woken up full of questions. If she gave him ten more minutes, he'd write down her social security number and run a background check. Then she'd crack like an egg.

She gathered the robe around her and pulled the sash tight against her middle. No need to have unexpected material slippage during her covert getaway.

As quietly as possible, she grabbed up her purse and folded the dress into as small a ball as she could. The crinoline made that task nearly impossible. Between the rustling and the big wad of white fabric that kept tumbling out of her arms, she was not off to the best start.

She bent her knees and felt for the briefcase below her. The damn thing was down on the floor somewhere. When her fingers brushed against the handle, she grabbed it up and tucked it under the yards of wedding dress. She'd come for the briefcase and whatever documents Jack kept hidden in there. She was leaving with the thing.

Time to go. With her hands full and her heart a little sore, she headed for the door. The light from the street lit her way as she tiptoed across the carpet and slipped her feet in her uncomfortable heels. She figured she must make quite a picture. Bathrobe, spiky shoes, an armful of white material. She'd be lucky if she didn't trip and break her neck. But she kept going.

The dramatic thing would have been to gaze over her shoulder with a wistful look. She was too practical for that. She'd carry enough reminders of their time together, of their night, without staring like a sick puppy at the bedroom door.

She reached for the doorknob. First she used her elbow, but the thing wouldn't turn. Then, with the briefcase and dress balanced against her thigh, she tried to pull. Pull and grab. Even shoved her hip against the thing to unstick whatever had gotten stuck. Nothing. She finally dropped her booty and twisted all the locks. Tried to open the door using every combination.

Still nothing.

"You can keep trying, but the door isn't going to open."

She winced at the sound of Jack's deep voice. Since she couldn't actually form a coherent sentence, she stayed quiet.

He didn't.

Thudding footsteps sounded behind her. He reached around and placed a palm on the door. "Did someone move the minibar to the hallway while I was asleep?"

She gulped down the panic threatening to overtake her and turned around. With her back to the door, she faced him and immediately regretted the move. He was as irresistible and adorable in the morning as he was at night.

His blue eyes flushed an even deeper, darker shade than normal. Those amazing lips that spent half the evening kissing her and whispering nonsense words in her ear were curled into a smile. "Going somewhere?"

"Uh, no."

"But you tried."

Why wasn't he angry? "Yeah, but—"

"This is one of those times that scientific progress we talked about failed. Miserably," he said.

He spoke English, but that wasn't helping her understand his point. "Huh?"

"The special alarm system I told you about malfunctioned."

"That's not good."

"The doors on the floor are locked and staying that way."

All sorts of responses shot around the inside of her brain. She went for the most obvious. Sticking with one-syllable responses seemed best. "What?"

"Trouble following the conversation?" He smiled at the thought.

She squeezed the items in her arms even tighter. "You could say that."

"A hotel employee knocked while you were asleep. A transformer blew at the construction site. When the electricity went out, the complex alarms went into shutdown mode. We have to wait until the system recycles. Should only be about twenty minutes or so."

She prayed for the electricity to turn back on right that second so she could bolt out the door and down the stairs. Hell, she'd settle for sliding down the garbage chute.

"Maintenance is working on the problem," he continued.

"Good. Uh, that's good."

He frowned. "Is it?"

"We can eat here, then."

He dropped his hand from the door but didn't move away. Wearing only a pair of striped lounge pants, he stood in front of her bare-chested and tan. All that sexy charm hovered right under the surface, but his face didn't give away his thoughts.

For some reason she wasn't afraid. Probably stupid, but physical violence wasn't the issue. His disappointment and the idea of being caught lying right to his face were.

First, she had to figure out just how angry he was this morning. "Still hungry?"

"Let me get this straight." He folded his arms across his middle. "You expect me to believe you were going in search of food in your bathrobe?"

"Sure." Why the hell not? He bought the pill thing. Maybe she could con her way out of this, too.

"With your wedding dress along for company?"

Okay, that made this excuse a bit harder. She struggled to find a reasonable explanation. Nothing came to her.

He pressed. "No comeback?"

"Not a good one."

"Not even a story you can dream up?"

If she was going out, she'd go out with a bang. "Surprisingly, no. Not at the moment, but I'm working on it."

"Okay." His shoulders fell.

The pressure building in the room eased back out. She didn't hear the hiss but felt it right down to her bones. "What does that mean?"

"You didn't come up with another lie. That's a start."

"You knew I was lying?"

"Yeah."

The man knew how to throw her off balance. "And you're not pissed off?"

"Let's say I'm used to it."

"Jack, if that's true, it's terrible. Why would people lie to you?"

"You tell me."

"Well, I . . ."

"Seeing you sneak out without even saying a word wasn't

the most flattering thing that's happened to me today. But, the day is young, so what can I say?"

Her time was running out. An angry bride was likely to be pacing the floor a few levels down. If only she could think of a reasonable way to leave and get that dress back. "Are you trying to tell me you're angry or not angry?"

"Let's say confused." He held out his hand to her.

"That makes two of us," she mumbled under her breath.

"Come back into the living room, Laine."

Now, that seemed like a bad idea. "But—"

"We have some things to talk about, don't you think?"

Her mind turned to mush. "Look, Jack—"

"We can talk here in the entry if you want, but we'd be more comfortable on the couch. And you look as if you're about to tip over. What all were you trying to drag into the hall with you?"

"Why aren't you angry?" She dropped then pushed the purse and briefcase to the side with her foot, hiding them both under the wedding dress.

Every cell in her body screamed at her to run. She couldn't do it. Instead, she slid her hand in his. At the touch, a warm sensation tingled up her arm, and everything inside her that had been jumping around at the speed of sound stilled.

"It's hard to be upset when I have no idea what's going on," he said as he led her back into the room and sat her down amid all the fluffy couch pillows. With his elbows balanced on his knees, he sat on the coffee table in front of her and faced her down.

"I suppose you want an explanation," she said.

"That would be a good start."

"Just how angry are you?" she asked. Always good to know that sort of thing before opening her mouth.

"At least you admit I have the right to be angry."

That was an understatement. More like furious or livid. Whatever words meant damn angry would work. "No."

His eyebrow shot up. "Really?"

"I didn't do anything to you."

"Actually, you did some amazing things to me, but let's stay focused on why you were trying to run out of here without saying goodbye," he said.

"Well—"

"—and why you were wearing a wedding dress when we met, when you obviously weren't on your way down the aisle."

She was a bit tired of his constant interrupting. "It's not that simple."

"I'm a smart guy, but use small words and I'll try to keep up."

"That's not what I meant," she said as she stalled for time.

"Then use big words and we'll try that."

"I'm working on a project," she blurted out before her brain caught up to her mouth.

He hesitated, then, "What kind?"

"I really can't talk about this, Jack. I should just go."

She tried to stand up, but he stopped her with a firm hand on her thigh. No pressure. Nothing hard or painful. Just his palm against her leg and a gentle squeeze that flooded her lower half with memories of sexy caresses between silky sheets. That he had that power over her frustrated her.

"There's nowhere to go, remember?" He pulled his hand back. "We're locked in, and there's no electricity even if you do manage to get into the hall."

"Have I mentioned how much I hate this hotel?"

"Don't blame the innocent hotel."

Speaking of science, her insides jumped around at the speed of light. "Science, then."

"That's because you're good at math and bad at science."

"Great at math, actually."

"Didn't mean to insult you."

"I'll live."

"Okay." He exhaled with a long, dramatic sound. "No more games, Laine. What's your last name?"

No harm in telling him that. "Monroe."

"Okay, Laine Monroe, tell me about this project. I'm looking for the who, what and why."

She mentally flipped through her options and realized she'd reached the end of the desperation card file. "I'm here to watch you."

"Watch me do what and did I need to be naked for this project?"

"No. That was a bonus." She wasn't exactly lying about that point.

"So, is the project about me or my tax returns?"

More gibberish. "What?"

He exhaled a second time. This one was longer and deeper than the first but equally dramatic. "I thought you were an accountant and financial guru. Not exactly the usual profession for following someone around Vegas."

"I am all that. Well, kind of. It's hard to explain." She stumbled over her words.

"We have all the time in the world, and I'm dying to know how an accountant becomes a spy."

*She loses a client's money, feels like crap and tries to make things right.* A little fact she kept to herself for now. "I was, past tense, an accountant. Now I'm unemployed and working on something private."

"Something that involves me."

"Sort of." More lies and half truths. As if she couldn't flip the switch from on to truth.

"What does that mean?"

"I can't tell you everything."

"Come on, honey, you're lousy at this spying stuff. Do I have to bring up the cramp medicine incident?"

"That was an accident." It was one thing for her to know how much she sucked at gathering information. It was a totally different thing for him to point it out.

"Let's get back to your project."

"No."

"Yes. What exactly are you supposed to be watching me do?"

She wasn't ready to leave their last conversation. "The cap flew off and the pills scattered. It happens."

"We're back on the pills?" When she nodded, he continued, "Not to normal people."

"I'm normal."

"We've somehow changed topics," he said.

"I haven't."

"You're losing focus."

"I'm mad at you," she blurted out.

"At me? Kind of have this backward, don't you?"

"Not the way I see it."

"I caught you trying to sneak out of my hotel room. In the who-gets-to-be-pissed contest, I'm ahead."

"If the door had worked—"

"I would have caught you in the hallway. I was watching from the bedroom and trying to figure out exactly why you went from my bed to a dead run in the other direction." A thread of anger moved into his voice.

For the first time she thought about the situation from his perspective. Sleep with a guy, run out and steal his briefcase in the bargain. Not exactly a stellar grade on his lovemaking skills, which were exceptional, but that wasn't the signal she sent out.

"One didn't have anything to do with the other."

"Let's start at the beginning. Did a groom really dump you this weekend?"

She answered because he asked a simple question. One

she could answer without breaking any confidentiality. "Well, no."

"Did you meet me by accident?"

"Uh, no." She tugged on her ear.

"So the scene at the blackjack table and later at the slots, all that was part of a plan?"

How did she explain that being with him was all for her? If she were being honest, she'd admit the attraction predated their meeting. She'd read all about him, studied him, and despite every terrible thing she'd heard, she felt a connection to him. Meeting him just strengthened the unseen bond.

She couldn't tell him that, but she needed him to know the intimacy was real. "I didn't sleep with you because of my project."

"That's a start."

"I wanted you to know that."

"Then, why?" His body braced as if waiting for a physical blow.

"Because I wanted to."

"For sex?" His voice broke on the question.

"No. It was more than sex, Jack."

"But it started as something else." He stood up and stalked to the window. "Why were you following me?"

She gave in. It wasn't as if she'd ever have another investigative job anyway. "See, we both know this guy."

"You're probably going to have to be more specific. I know a lot of people."

"In business."

His shoulders slumped. "Shit. You mean Mark."

*Crap!* "How did you get Mark from that statement?"

"Am I wrong?"

"Uh, what name did you say again?"

"Nice try." He wiped a hand through his hair. "Mark Rudolph. My partner. How do you know him?"

"I really can't—"

"Laine." He pressed a hand against the glass.

A wave of memories flooded back to her. Last night. Touching him. Taking control and enjoying her power over his body. Sliding down on him as he pulsed inside her. Later, rolling across the carpet before he took her again.

Those moments together, feeling and not thinking, meant everything to her. Jack brought out the sensual creature in her. He made her laugh. Showed her satisfaction both on a bedroom level and on an intellectual level.

Now she'd never know if they could have had something. A relationship built on deceit didn't have a shot. Her head knew that, but the rest of her body lagged a step behind.

He turned back around but didn't move from the window. "I know Mark's accountant. He's fifty and bald. You're not him."

"Maybe there are things you don't know about Mark." Like the fact he took business funds and hid them from Jack because he worried about missing money from the business and had to know if he could trust Jack before he put the money back. The same money her bosses stole when they stole everyone else's money in the firm.

"It's hard to believe there's something else I don't know about Mark."

"What?"

"Did Mark tell you the part about his prescription drug addiction?" he asked.

The words sliced through her. No. That couldn't be true. "His . . . ?"

"He's messed up, Laine. Really messed up."

Sure, Mark was upset. Despondent even, but all of that was over Jack and his possible complicity in something illegal. "That's not true."

"Because he doesn't seem like the type?"

Well, yeah. "He was fine. Completely coherent."

"I'm not sure that's the addiction test," he said.

"Then what is?"

"How about the fact his wife, a medical doctor, nearly lost her license when Mark used her prescription pad to write phony scripts."

"That's terrible."

"Or how he ended up in the emergency room when someone gave him tainted drugs."

"I didn't know—"

"Or about the hundred thousand he took from our business that I can't track down. That's on top of the tens of thousands that have disappeared bit by bit over the last few months."

That was the exact amount of money Mark had given her. "He took the money?"

"He made it disappear. I don't know where it is."

This wasn't possible. If what Jack said was true, then she not only lost her career and her dignity when the regulators closed down her old office, but she also lost her ability to read people.

"Everything checked out," she mumbled. "He was the owner of a business."

"Right, the co-owner of Micron Industries. You just slept with the other owner."

This could not be happening. "Why do you think he took the money?"

Jack shook his head as a look of sadness moved into his eyes. "He used the stolen money to fund his habits and to make up for the shortfall at home when the checking account went dry. His wife got hit with a temporary suspension. He panicked."

"Why didn't he come to you?"

"I've asked myself that a hundred times. I don't know."

He looked so tired, as if the sparkle that lit his bright

blues eyes had been snuffed out. Damn, had she done that or had Mark?

One thing still didn't make sense. "If you were having all this trouble at the office, why are you in Las Vegas?"

"I got out of town while my P.I. finished his investigation and found the evidence on Mark's money trail." He sat down on the edge of the coffee table. "Figured I'd take a couple of days and decide how I'm going to handle the information once I get back."

"Oh."

"I haven't heard anything yet." He stared at her, as if waiting for her to give the right answer. "Care to make the job easier and tell me where the money is?"

She hated every minute of this conversation. "I can't—"

"Divulge a client's financial information. Yeah, I get it."

She placed her hand on his knee, hoping the contact would give him some comfort. Or at least make her feel better about delivering her news. "I can only go by what Mark told me about the money."

"Which was?"

"A lie, I guess." She didn't really have to guess. She knew. She could see it all now. All the pieces fit. "That you were overextended. That Mark had to shift some funds to make sure he could make payroll if you dipped into the till again."

"Figured it was something like that."

What a mess. A mess she helped create. How could she tell him she lost the money?

"Are you going to press charges?"

"He's a friend, Laine. An old friend. He's lost his way, but I'm not going to abandon him now."

She hated to ask, but she had to do it. "Now what?"

"About what?"

"With us?" That's the only thing she really cared about.

"We'll see if we can get this door fixed so you can go back to wherever it was you were really going a few minutes ago." He flashed a sad smile. "I've never kept a woman against her will in my life. I'm not going to start now."

"Jack—"

"It's time for you to go."

# Chapter Eight

A half hour later the lights snapped on.

Laine left soon after the electricity blinked to life. He missed her a minute later. She was as addictive as gambling. Sure, he made it possible for her to leave. He just never expected she would.

Damn women.

An apology would have been nice. Maybe she could have managed a second or two of hesitation before walking out the door. A little groveling while he took the moral high ground and decided whether or not to trust her.

Nope. Nothing. Nada.

He'd opened the door for her and watched her leave dressed in nothing but a bathrobe and dragging her wedding dress behind her. Damn women. Who needed them? Not him. Finding companionship had never been an issue before, and it wouldn't be now. Next time he'd keep the talking to a minimum. Hard to form a connection, other than physical, without talking.

For a second he'd thought he found that extra piece with Laine. That elusive part that reached beyond the bedroom and into something deeper. Then she'd walked out and taken that spark of hope with her.

He plunked down on his couch and knocked back the

most expensive tiny drink of his life out of a minibar bottle. A soft whirl of the air conditioner filled the silence as it kicked back to life.

The same silence that had returned the minute she left.

Damn . . . not women. A woman. Singular. Laine.

Mark's disloyalty arose out of addiction. Laine didn't have that excuse. She'd screwed him in every way possible and didn't offer a twelve-step program for recovery. He closed his eyes and let his head drop back against the couch.

Sitting in the bedroom didn't work. The sheets carried her scent. So did his bathroom. He had to escape to the living room to forget about her. That sure as hell wasn't working.

If he tried really hard, he could block out the feel of her silky skin and the sound of her smoky voice. The way she made him feel both in and out of bed. Lighter and relaxed and ready to take on any challenge.

He concentrated on building that mental wall against her. Then something clicked in his brain. His eyelids popped open, and he stared at the ceiling, trying to figure out the reason for the uneasy feeling moving through him.

The briefcase.

His head flew forward, and he looked around the room.

"She took my fucking briefcase."

He threw a shirt over his lounge pants and slipped on his dress shoes to run down the hall to the elevator. After a ride that lasted forever, he hit the casino. The floor buzzed with activity despite the early hour. The lure of electricity and expensive lattes brought people downstairs in droves.

There was a healthy mix of happy people and complainers milling about. Amazing how the whiners always talked so much louder than the rest of the crowd.

He reached the front desk and asked for Laine.

Then asked again.

Then a third time.

"Sorry." The clerk refused, for the fourth time, to provide any information on Laine. Casino policy and all that.

Screw policy. Time to use some financial muscle. "Where's Alex?"

"We haven't seen Mr. Mitchell since the lights went out."

"How is that possible? He runs the place."

"We're looking, sir." Her tone was a bit sharper that time.

"Fine. Anyone else I can talk to?" There had to be some perks for dropping a wad of cash in this place every quarter.

"I can ring Ms. Monroe's room for you." The perky blonde smiled so wide he wondered if she had extra teeth stuffed in that mouth.

"Fine," he said through clenched teeth.

After several rounds of keyboard clicking the clerk spoke again. "Oh, wait. She just checked out. Sorry."

"When?"

"Mr. MacAllister, I can't—"

"When?" He slapped the desk. "Never mind. I'll find her."

Laine either came from town, which he doubted since she didn't seem to know one single thing about Las Vegas, or from his hometown. Last he checked San Diego was part of Southern California, and for Mark to go to her, she must work nearby. Either way, she'd be headed for the main entrance where both the cab line and the garage were located. For once, he hoped for a long line.

He took off at a run, slipping as his hotel-provided shoes slid against the marble floor. He dodged through casino patrons, nearly knocking over a slim brunette in a blur of impossibly high heels.

"Hey!"

"Sorry!" he called over his shoulder but didn't stop. More than likely only minutes separated them.

Past the poker tables and expensive gift shop. He hit the

slick floor of the lobby and slid to a stop. She stood right in front of the ornate revolving door to the outside. The wedding dress was gone, but she still had her bag and his briefcase.

"Laine!"

Her head whipped around, and she mouthed something that looked suspiciously like "Oh, shit." Now he'd get an explanation. The fact she appeared to be frozen to the spot on the floor would help.

Pushing through a group of people wearing identical blue T-shirts, he moved in. She did some shuffling of her own. She didn't take off, but she did lean over and talk to a burly guy in a burgundy blazer.

"Laine, wait right there."

Mr. No-Neck stepped right in front of him. "Sir, that's far enough."

"What? Get the hell out of my way." He looked around the security guard, which was a lot like trying to see around a building.

Laine sprinted for the door.

"Stop!"

"Sir, that's enough."

"Enough what?" Jack tried to sidestep the monster, but the monster had other ideas.

"That's it." The guard talked into his closed fist, then turned his attention back to Jack. "The lady wants to be left alone."

"What the hell are you talking about?" He barely got the sentence out when the burgundy swarm hit him.

They came from every direction, each one bigger than the one before. And, they were on him in a flash, like being smashed with bricks. Three-hundred-pound bricks.

"Damn it!" Those were the last words he uttered before he hit the hard floor with his arms pinned behind his back and his dignity spilled all over the expensive tile.

"Settle down, sir." They stayed polite as they wrestled him down.

"What are you doing?" he shouted, but they ignored his growing fury.

"Subduing you, sir. The lady asked for help."

"The lady stole my briefcase, you asshole."

He felt the grip on his forearms loosen. "Sir?"

"I'm staying in this hotel. Ask Alex."

"He's not here, sir."

"Then let me up so I can show you my key and before I sue your sorry asses."

They tried to help him to his feet, but he shook off their hands. Racing through the door, he saw the long cab line and no Laine. Too late. She was gone.

Part of the burgundy brigade parked right behind him. "Sir?"

"What?" he barked out.

"I need to see that key."

Jack reached in his pocket to prove his identity and realized he didn't have a pocket. The key was back in his wallet, which was back in his room.

*Damn woman.*

# Chapter Nine

Seventy-two hours later Laine walked into Jack's office suite ready to demand a meeting. She wanted him to know what she'd found out. She wanted to see him.

Starting this afternoon, her new job search would begin. If that failed, her new solo accountant agency would open. With her former bosses in jail for defrauding clients, her list of options included only a few items. Their taint had passed to her and threatened to ruin whatever job prospects she still had, but she refused to back down.

The resumé brought her thoughts back to Jack. Hell, her coffee cup made her think of Jack. She couldn't shake his image from her head. She continued to plug his name into her Internet search engine and look him up. She snuck peeks at the newspaper article she kept near her bed. The one that included his photo.

Yeah, she defined pathetic.

Would he ever understand she'd stolen the briefcase to help him? Sure, it was stupid and spur-of-the-moment, as stupid and spur-of-the-moment things usually are.

She'd had some dumb idea about earning his trust, since he'd made it clear trust was a big-ticket item for him. She wanted to prove she could help. Stealing his briefcase hadn't been the best start to that plan, but she'd needed his personal information. Needed a reason to find him again later.

Part of her wanted to see if he'd look for her. The answer so far was no. She'd wallow in that later. Right now she had an appointment with Jack. He just didn't know it yet.

"Laine Monroe here to see Jack MacAllister." She wore her smart black pantsuit and light blue silk shirt. She was the essence of professionalism.

If this failed, she'd find another wedding dress.

"Is Mr. MacAllister expecting you?" An attractive assistant of about fifty smiled at her.

Laine knew by instinct this woman would wrestle her to the ground and put her in a headlock to protect Jack.

"Yes."

The assistant's perfectly plucked eyebrow arched. "I don't think so."

Yeah, well, she tried. "He'll see me."

"He's very busy this afternoon. Maybe we can set up something for next week with one of his managers."

Next week she'd be at home staring at his photo like a goofball. No, now was the time. "Please announce me."

"She doesn't have to."

Jack's deep voice sounded from behind Laine. When she turned around, she saw him standing in the hallway to the office with his hands wrapped around an extra large coffee mug and a slim stack of folders.

"Jack."

"Laine."

Silence.

Tick, tick, tick.

More silence.

She wondered if the meeting could possibly be more awkward. "I need to talk with you."

"Mr. MacAllister—"

He raised his hand to cut off his assistant's help. "It's okay, Pam. Ms. Monroe and I have a few things to discuss."

She would have smirked in triumph, despite the immaturity of that action, but her tongue stuck to the roof of her mouth. Jack looked even better now, settled on his home turf beneath rows of washed-out watercolor paintings and dark traditional furniture.

He opened his office door and motioned for her to go inside. "After you."

The pain at seeing him replaced the pain of missing him. Watching him now, wearing faded jeans and a plain white oxford, broke something cold and frozen inside of her. All those feelings of loss and shame inundated her.

"Is this a casual day?" She asked the question to mask her discomfort. "I'm not used to seeing you in jeans."

"Technically, you've seen me mostly without clothing."

The reminder sent a flush of heat racing down her body. "Until the lights went out."

"As for the dress code, we believe in a relaxed environment. If my folks go outside or have a meeting, they dress for the part."

Why were they talking about clothes? "I see."

He dropped into his oversized leather chair and propped his feet on the desk. For some reason he looked more at ease here than he did on his vacation in Las Vegas.

"Have a seat." He motioned to the chair across from him.

She ignored the offer. She sensed she needed to stay on her feet to keep up with this conversation. She stood across from him, on the other side of his huge walnut desk, feeling a bit as if she'd been called to the principal's office.

"What are you doing here, Laine? I'm assuming the visit is not to ask about my wardrobe."

"I need to talk to you."

"I'm listening."

The softness in his voice encouraged her. She took a deep breath and plowed ahead. "I have news about Mark."

"Really?" He dropped his feet to the floor and sat up straight.

"After our time in Las Vegas—"

"Is that what we're calling it?"

She ignored the interruption. "I did some digging. You were right. Mark did give me your money. Then, my bosses lost your money. Rather, they stole it. It's all right here."

She slid a folder of newspaper articles and documents across the desk at him. When he didn't say anything or reach for the file, she continued. "Money is my specialty. I'm helping the authorities trace my old firm's business dealings. Seems they set up a dummy file and some phony records. They siphoned off the money, just as Mark had done to you. It's some sort of justice, I guess."

"I see."

"I was also able to look at some of Mark's personal records. I'm trying to trace those as well. I have gotten this so far—"

"How did you get his personal financial records exactly?"

Illegally. Through back channels. By pulling in every favor she owed on the planet. By begging Mark's wife to help her. From Jack's briefcase.

And she did it all for him.

"You had some and I have my sources," she said.

"Such as?"

"Stop interrupting." She slid another folder in his direction. "Here it is."

He ignored that one, too.

"I see," he said.

Her temper blew. "What the hell do you see?"

He hesitated, his face blank but his eyes as intelligent and watchful as ever. "That's quite a temper."

"I'm only getting started."

"Then, let's cut right to it, shall we? Mark checked into a rehab program this morning. We staged an intervention, and he broke down and went."

His deep voice hypnotized her into falling in the chair without thinking. Her wobbly legs couldn't hold her upright anymore anyway.

"Really?"

"Yeah, really."

"Is he okay?"

"He hasn't been okay in a long time, Laine, but now he has a chance."

"That's great news."

"Great is too strong."

"So. I'm wasting my time helping with Mark's records?"

"No." He grinned that sexy grin that made her insides all gooey. "Your information saves me a lot of digging time. Thanks. Never had anyone try to save me before."

"Seems to me you're a guy in need of some saving." In need of someone he could trust. She wanted to be that someone.

He frowned. "I said I appreciate what you did."

Now she had his appreciation. Lucky for her. "Then I guess I'll go."

"No."

"No?"

"I have some questions for you." He stood up and walked around until he leaned against the desk in front of her.

She had to look up to talk to him and didn't care for the vulnerable sensation one bit. "Such as?"

"You weren't the only one digging around in other people's business."

That sounded bad. "Fill me in, Jack."

"My investigator. He's had some trouble getting the scoop on you but finally nailed most of it down."

"Why?"

"Well, he's had something like twenty years of experience at this job. He has certifications hanging on his wall."

"Not that." She dug her fingernails into the arms of the chair. "I don't care about his resumé. I care about why he's looking into me in the first place. You plan on pressing charges against me or something?"

His gazed traveled over her face. "You're worried I'm still pissed off about the casino security thing."

"Among other things."

He shrugged, but his smile never faltered. "Yeah, well, I won't lie to you. I wasn't happy. It's been years since someone slammed my head into the floor."

"You're exaggerating."

"No, I'm not. I have the injuries to prove it."

"Oh."

"Convincing the meathead security crew I was staying in the hotel wasn't exactly easy either since I left my key, and my pants, in the room when I went to find you."

Her hand flew to her mouth to hide her chuckle. "Oh, Jack. That's terrible."

"Apparently, after all they had to deal with during the blackout, they lost their collective sense of humor."

"I really am sorry." She meant it.

"For what?"

Every damn thing. For leaving him. For losing him. "Sending them after you."

"Hmmm."

Typically cryptic. "You don't believe me?"

"I don't care about the security guards. I care about the lying and stealing," he said.

He read off her major sins, and every word plunged into her with the force of an ice pick. "I can explain."

"Let me try to do it for you." He folded his hand over

hers with a touch so loving and sweet she almost fell out of her chair.

"How are you going to tell me what I did to you?" she asked. "Isn't that my job?"

He kissed her open palm. "Actually, you lost your job, in desperation got lured in by Mark's lies and then used me in a misguided attempt to fix everyone else's problems."

She tried to talk over the shivers racing through her. "You got all that from your P.I. in two days?"

"I told you he was good." He rubbed his thumb over the back of her hand and treated her palm to another kiss.

He knew everything. About the scandal. She tried to remove her hand, but he held on. "About my firm—"

He stopped her with a finger over her lips. "I know you didn't defraud clients."

"You, but . . . how?"

"You're a terrible liar."

She thought about getting indignant until she realized that was probably a weird compliment. "Thanks. I think."

"To me, that's quite a compliment." He kissed her knuckles in that way that made her knees weak. "I love that about you."

"That I suck at lying? You're a very strange man."

He chuckled. "Of course, you still do have my briefcase." Not a question. A statement.

Something inside her deflated. She struggled to find the right words to tell him how rotten the last two days had been without him, and he was worried about his property. "Uh, sure. At home."

"Good."

"Is that why you sent the investigator after me?" When he didn't answer, she lifted her head and stared at him. "Jack?"

"No."

That bubble popped to life again. "No?"

"At first, I was going to do something male and stupid and offer you an accountant job here with me. Seemed fair after all we'd been through."

"Like a payment for services rendered? A roll in the sack equals one job offer?" That burned her, and her voice increased in volume as a result.

"Yeah, that."

"I would have told you to go to hell."

"And I would have deserved it." The gentle rubbing against her hand turned into a massage.

"We agree on something." All the wrong things, but at least he didn't insult her like that.

He talked about job opportunities when she wanted to hear about him. About them. About whether he was willing to give her a second chance. Showing, once again, they weren't on the same page.

"It wouldn't have worked anyway," he said.

"Because I would have castrated you with my hand had you even suggested such a thing."

He laughed, the sound open and carefree. "Feisty as ever, I see."

"Pompous as hell, I see," she shot back.

"Let's start again." He tugged her to her feet and brought her to stand between his thighs.

"Jack!"

"Shh. Just listen." His palms settled on her hips. "You couldn't work for me because I have a strict policy against dating employees, and we are most definitely going to be dating."

Did he just say dating? "You?"

"Yeah, me. Who else would I want you to date?"

She put her hands on his cheeks. "Jack, make sense."

"I know it sounds like a high school term, but I wasn't

sure what else to call it. Thought we'd start there and see where we go."

"Go?" she choked out the question.

"My preference is to start with living together, then move on, but I figured I'd let you get used to the idea first."

"Living . . . ?"

"I think we could go all the way."

His boyish grin nearly did her in. "After everything I did, you want to date?" Or more?

His hands slid behind her back as he pulled her close. "You tried to help. You sucked at it, but you tried. I know the bedroom and the conversation were real. You won't lie to me, unless it's in a misguided attempt to help me."

"True."

"But you're not going to lie to me ever again, right?"

"Yes."

"We had a connection worth exploring."

Her hands plunged through his hair. If she didn't kiss him soon, she'd burst. "It was real."

"I know."

"Really, Jack, it was."

He rolled his eyes. "See, when I say 'I know,' that means I agree with you. You can stop arguing at that point."

She wrapped her arms around his neck. "But, we like to argue."

"There are other things I like better." He nuzzled his nose against hers.

"Such as?"

He leaned back, taking her with him. Her feet lifted right off the floor, and her lower body pressed against his erection.

"Jack!" She sprawled on top of him in the middle of that huge desk, knocking paperwork and the stapler to the floor.

"What?" he asked, the very picture of innocent charm.

"We can't do this."

"I'm the boss." How reasonable he sounded.

"What if your assistant walks in?"

"She wouldn't dare."

"I can't—"

He pressed his midsection against hers. "I'm sure I can. But I have one question for you."

He kissed her, unleashing all of his pent-up need and desire and igniting hers. She was breathless when she came back up for air.

"Yes, whatever it is, yes."

"Do you feel lucky?" he asked with a sparkle in his beautiful blue eyes.

She threw her head back and laughed. "I believe I do."

# PLAYER'S CLUB

# Chapter One

"Just as I thought." An annoying tsk-tsking sound followed the comment. "We have a good deal of work ahead of us."

At the sound of the bored female voice, Zach Jacobs stopped what he was doing, which happened to be lying on his desk on top of the hottest blond waitress on the Las Vegas Strip. His companion wore the Berkley Hotel and Casino cocktail uniform like a second skin. She'd also made it clear not ten minutes before that he had a green light for action; all he had to do was drive on through.

Then the nasty traffic cop entered the room.

The same one standing at his door clicking her tongue against her teeth, creating one of the most annoying sounds on the planet. The one talking to him, and not in the good way. The one most decidedly not screaming his name out in ecstasy, despite his every effort to the contrary.

Jenna Barrister. Erection killer.

He swiveled around in time to see Jenna walk in the room with her black-and-thin-white-line-striped suit, bare toned legs, sexy shoes and . . . yep, there it was. A shiny metal clipboard.

Every time he looked at her, which was as often as possible, he wondered how a woman so damn hot could be so fucking evil. He suddenly had the urge to rip the eight-by-eleven thing out of her perfectly manicured fingers and throw it out of the window. With any luck, she'd dive out after it.

"The door was locked," he said, stating the obvious.

"I have a key," Jenna responded, oblivious to the obvious.

Fine. He'd be more clear. "Get out."

Demanding that Jenna leave was worth a try. He'd tried everything else with her, but the hotel's outside consultant appeared to be immune to everything he threw her way. His anger. His tantrums. His flirting. He could understand her not falling at his feet the minute he turned on the charm, but, come on, would it kill her not to laugh when he tried to make a move?

"I'm not ready to leave yet," she said as she walked around the small room, scowling at the piles of paperwork scattered on the floor.

She came to a halt right beside the desk. From his position, he could see her lean, tanned legs.

"This is private." He tried to get up, but his arms and legs wouldn't move. It was as if the sound of Jenna's husky voice and unexpected visit froze him in place.

His companion wasn't exactly jumping up either. Anika lay under him like a rag doll, her eyes big and her mouth hanging open. When they dated previously, Anika never made this face. The stunned look was new. And he understood exactly how Anika felt. Jenna had that effect on him, too.

Jenna squatted down until she was eye-level with his desk and the tiny space between their bodies. The space where his withering erection happened to be. "Interesting."

"Happy you think so. Now, get out."

"I mean, it's interesting you decided to have sex with a

member of the staff right on top of my memo which specifically outlines how you are not to have sex with the staff."

"You've sent fifty memos in the month since you got here. If I read them all, I wouldn't have time to cook."

"Twelve, and I've been here three weeks and four days." She scribbled something down on her notepad.

"Guess it only feels like fifty," he mumbled as he tried to see whatever it was she found important enough to write down.

"Do you have sex on top of all of my memos? If so, I can ask your staff to read them to you before they put them on your desk."

"I . . ." That was it. Nothing else came to him. Probably had something to do with her saying "staff" repeatedly.

"Some would consider your conduct, shall we say, ballsy."

Staff. Balls. The woman needed a new vocabulary. "You think that—"

"Or maybe she doesn't work here." Jenna's gaze wandered over what she could see of Anika, which wasn't much since he was plastered against the stunned woman from thigh to shoulder. "Is she just borrowing a staff uniform for a role-playing sex exercise perhaps?"

She needed to stop saying "staff" or his head would explode. "If you would just leave—"

"At least your clothes are still on." She started scribbling again. "For now."

"Do I get points for that? If so, write that down. I want all the credit I can get."

"Not really. Probably just a slowness issue on your part. If I had come in three or four minutes later, the clothing likely would be elsewhere. On the floor, maybe?"

Slow? Now she was knocking his technique. The woman could destroy a mood faster than a story about dead cats.

"How can I put this? Yeah, let's try this: get the hell out of my office!"

"Thank you, but no." Jenna leaned in and tapped the tip of her pen against Anika's shoulder, making the poor woman yelp in surprise. "And you are?"

Anika's gaze flew back and forth between them. "Uhh . . . I'm . . ."

"That's none of your business." He shifted up to his elbows. He would have gotten off the desk, but Jenna's hovering made that impossible. He had to stay where he was or risk landing on Jenna, tempting as that was. "And while you're at it, get out."

"Still no." Jenna cleared her throat.

"What do I have to do to get rid of you?" He really wanted to know what he had to do to get her under him, but he wasn't about to ask that question.

"Do you know her name?"

Anika stared at him. Stared at Jenna. Stared at the ceiling. Then burst into tears.

"Now look what you did." Jenna patted Anika's head, likely because that was the woman's only visible body part underneath him.

"Me? What did I do?" He hadn't done anything. Hadn't had time. That was kind of the point.

"Isn't it obvious?" Jenna turned her attention back to Anika. "He can't be that bad at this. He actually has quite the reputation as a ladies' man. That's why I'm here."

"To kill my reputation?" he asked.

"To eliminate your sexual escapades."

"Wait a minute."

"Or is the problem that he's crushing you?" Jenna looked at Anika, then frowned at him. "Maybe you should get off the nice lady."

"Jenna."

"Yes?"

"Don't push me."

"Fine."

"Fine?"

"Sure. I can be accommodating. Take your time." She tapped that pen against her clipboard. "I'll wait."

She wanted to watch? "What?"

"Really, how long can this take?" She looked at the skinny watch on her wrist. "Six, maybe seven, minutes?"

"Jenna—"

"I can sit over"—she turned around in a circle, taking in every inch of the room—"well, there really isn't a place to sit. This place looks more like a men's locker room than an office."

"Jenna!"

"I'll look out the window. Go ahead. Finish up."

"Have you lost your mind?" He had. No question. Whatever brain cells he had this morning were long gone. Scared off by Jenna and her man-killing tactics.

"You're right. I have other things to do."

"Terrorize small animals, perhaps?"

"I'll give you a half hour to do whatever it is you have planned here"—she waved her hand in the air in a dismissive gesture that killed whatever was left of his libido—"then you really need to get off this young woman and get back to work."

She acted as if there was still a chance something might happen. Not likely. His penis might never recover from this scene. "Or what, Jenna?"

She talked right over him. "I need to get some notes from my office. I'll call to reschedule our appointment." With that, she took off for the door.

A smart man would have let her go. Not him. He just kept coming back for more. Had since the first time he met her almost four weeks ago. Saw her. Wanted her. Propositioned her. Then nursed his wounded ego when she laughed at him. He'd been in a holding pattern and constant state of arousal ever since.

"We didn't have a meeting today," he called after her.

"Consider me your standing appointment."

"Like hell."

She chuckled to herself. "I guess that would make this woman your lying appointment."

He'd lost all control of the situation, but kept trying to get it back. "Jenna—"

"You'll hear from me soon."

He took that as the threat it was.

# Chapter Two

Zach's last day as playboy chef for the Berkley Hotel and Casino's most prestigious restaurant had arrived. He just didn't know it yet. Starting today there would be a new Zach Jacobs. One who followed the rules. One who confined his cooking to the kitchen.

Berkley's management staff had brought her in from the outside to assess all aspects of the hotel, in general, and look into the concerns of a disgruntled male guest whose wife took a particular interest in Zach, in particular. After about a week she knew the problem: Zach. She needed to fix him.

As a consultant, she had free rein. Since, thanks to his culinary reputation, firing Zach was out of the question, she would take another tact. Remake him.

Kind of like trying to stop a runaway bus, but she wasn't about to back down.

She wanted a permanent position at Berkley. No more traveling. No more moving around. She wanted a real home for once in her life. A stable in-house job with benefits and a desk. She needed Zach for that. Zach with his zipper up and concentration solely on food preparation. After seeing him in action yesterday, she wondered if anyone could do this job.

A runaway bus would be an easier job.

She leaned back in her soft leather chair and nearly tipped over thanks to the loose seat. She grabbed on to the desktop for balance, then buzzed the temporary secretary the hotel had assigned her. "Please ask Mr. Jacobs to report to my office."

After a beat of silence the twenty-something assistant with the shiny blond hair and cannonball-sized breasts—the same ones that must have cost three months' salary—answered. "Uh, Ms. Bartholomew?"

"The name is Barrister, Andrea. I told you yesterday and almost every day before that." She thought the constant corrections would have driven the point home, but dearest Andrea still wasn't getting it.

"Right. But, see, it's almost six. I go home at six."

"It's five-thirty. You can make one telephone call in thirty minutes."

After three weeks on the job and another month investigating the problem and sitting in on meetings before that, she'd heard enough about Zach and his considerable talent in and out of the bedroom to last a lifetime. Hell, yesterday a wealthy female guest had demanded his home telephone number. Apparently she thought Zach counted as an amenity she could order from housekeeping. For all Jenna knew, maybe he was.

The intercom buzzed back. "Um, Ms. Bartholomew?"

"Still Barrister."

"Right. Well, Zach said no."

Her frustration with Andrea moved to Zach. "Excuse me?"

"He said if you want him, you'll need to come and get him."

She could almost hear the smirk in Zach's voice when he delivered that line. "Fine, Andrea. Thank you."

Not fine. Not fine at all. If Zach wanted a command performance on his home turf, she'd oblige. She stood up and fastened the middle button on her jacket to cover her silky camisole. She should have worn pants to kick Zach's butt all over the hotel but, for some reason, had opted for a matching short skirt and T-strap high heels.

At five-seven, with long legs and a body shaped by hours of laps in the pool, she knew she looked damn good for twenty-eight. There was some juvenile satisfaction in showing Zach what he couldn't have while telling him the new rules.

She stepped into her outer office. "I'm going to the kitchen."

"To see Zach?"

"No, Andrea, to get a piece of pie." She sighed when the other woman looked confused. "Yes, to see Zach."

"Oh." Andrea toyed with the tiny white button struggling to hold her thin sweater together across those gigantic breasts.

Jenna reached the door, portfolio in hand, and turned back to Andrea. "You better set up a meeting with Alex Mitchell for later this evening. Say, in about an hour."

She started to walk away again, but Andrea stopped her. "Uh, Ms. Bartholomew?"

In ten more minutes she'd figure out a way to tattoo her name on Andrea's wrinkle-free forehead. "My name didn't change in the last three minutes, Andrea. It's Barrister."

"Sure. Right. So, why do you need the meeting?"

So she could explain to the assistant manager what she planned for the casino's top-rated, Five-Diamond, award-winning chef. "Just do it."

Jenna marched down the long, wide hallways that led from the executive suite to the kitchen of the casino's finest restaurant. Zach's domain.

She pushed open one of the two swinging doors and walked into a scene that could only be described as controlled chaos. Shiny metal surfaces, stacks of dishes and dozens of people all dressed in black pants and white cooking smocks running back and forth.

Zach stood right in the dead center chopping green stalks of something vegetablelike with a huge knife made for delivering death. She made a mental note to make sure the knife wasn't in his hand when she told him what was about to happen.

"Zach." Somehow her soft voice cut through the bustle, and everyone stopped to stare at her. Including Zach, who looked up and treated her to that dimpled pretty-boy smile. The one with the added superpower of melting women's resistance in a single glance.

"Ah, Jenna. Slumming it in my humble kitchen?"

Interesting Zach thought thousands of dollars of kitchen equipment looked humble. "I need to see you."

His eyebrow lifted. "You want to see more of me than you are right now?"

She heard a low mumbling of voices and more than a few chuckles behind her but ignored them. She tried to disregard Zach's warm voice, too. A chef should be fat and dumpy, maybe a bit nutty from the constant food buzz and high intake of sugar.

Not Zach. His short, dark hair hovered somewhere between black and brown. Those chocolate brown eyes and that smooth, deep tan mixed with a long, lean body highlighting the devious charm like that of the frat boy she fell for in college before she knew better.

The package in every sense, objective or otherwise, worked. Zach possessed the looks to go with that sinful reputation and a love of women that bordered on the extreme. No prima donna attitude here.

Women shoved room keys into his pockets and asked for private tasting parties with him. Fellow female employees waited in line for a turn with the skillful stud. One or two of the anorexic-looking ones even managed to choke down some food around him.

She'd seen him on day two on the job and hadn't been able to wipe his image from her mind since. But that didn't have anything to do with her task today. Their meeting, like their relationship, was all work and no play.

"I need to talk with you," she repeated.

"Now's not the best time. You need to come back later."

There would never be a good time. And he was done calling the shots. "Whatever you're doing can wait."

"I'm setting up for the dinner rush and finalizing the plans for the Douglas wedding tomorrow. So, no, not a good time."

"I'm sure your"—she gestured around the room—"staff can handle everything without you."

He stopped in midchop. That devilish smile grew even wider. "You keep referring to my staff. Is there something I should know?"

Yeah, that she was about to cut it off. Not literally, of course. "Now."

He wiped his hands on the towel hanging around his waist and put the knife down on the stainless steel countertop with a thud. "You were saying?"

He was pushing her, and she was about to shove back. "Do I need to define 'now' for you?"

He stared at her for a beat longer than necessary, then clapped. "Listen up, *staff*. Jenna and I have a few things to discuss. Everybody stay focused. I'll be back in two minutes. Sam, you're in charge."

He slipped off his chef tunic, leaving behind only a slim gray T-shirt that outlined every muscle across his chest and black jeans that showcased everything else.

Damn, did the guy lift refrigerators in his spare time? Wielding a knife couldn't build those muscles. No, a body like that took good genes and a lot of practice. No wonder women threw their room keys at him. Hell, she was toying with the idea.

He looked at her, all his attention focused on her. "Something wrong?"

Him. Her. Everything. "Of course not."

"Good. We'll use my office."

After what she saw in there yesterday—or almost saw—his office was not her first choice, but she didn't have many alternatives if she wanted privacy. The deafening silence and interested stares coming from the rest of the white-shirt brigade suggested they needed privacy for this conversation.

He walked into his cramped office and jumped up on his metal desk. "What's up?"

"This room still is a disaster." Papers sat in piles on the very edges of his desk, just waiting for an excuse to leap off. Cookbooks and boxes littered the floor. Other than his wooden desk chair, there wasn't anywhere to sit in the room.

His gaze followed hers around the room. "I'm a cook, not a housekeeper."

"You weren't exactly cooking last time I saw you in here."

"Depends on how you define cooking." He wiggled his eyebrows.

He talked as if he were twenty, not thirty-three. "That's an interesting thing to say to someone who is here to assess your work ethic."

"I don't think of you that way."

"How do you think of me?"

He braced his arms on either side of his thighs with his hands curled around the desk's edge. "You probably don't want to know. Look, my time's limited here. What do you need, Jenna?"

The question, so soft and deep, carried a double meaning, and she bet he knew it. He came off as a carefree guy with no obvious skills other than what he could do with a spatula. She knew differently.

Zach had graduated from Yale with a degree in business, and culinary school had come after. The director of Human Resources warned her not to be taken in by Zach's good looks or to think everything he accomplished stemmed from luck. He was a tough and determined businessman who happened to have an incredible talent for cooking. The lazy façade was just that. Fake.

"I'll cut to the chase," she said.

He swept his arm out in a dramatic gesture. "By all means, cut."

She'd heard he liked it fast and hard. Apparently that referred to everything in his life. "The company—"

"The CIA?"

"No, the company that pays you."

"My mistake." He waved her on. "Go ahead."

"The company believes your behavior has gotten out of control. Human Resources has been spending a great deal of time cleaning up after you. As such, I've been hired to help you."

His big grin faltered a bit. "I haven't made a mess since I was five."

"There are those who would disagree." Like her, for instance.

"Fine. Then I'll fix my own mess."

"Yes, well, unless and until the hotel can find another superstar who just happens to be named Zach, it's stuck with you as its super chef."

"Lucky for me my parents didn't name me Fred."

She ignored the joke. "I've been assigned to watch you."

"Any body part in particular?"

That was a different list. One she didn't intend to share. "Watch over you."

"You're some kind of corporate baby-sitter?"

"I'm starting to think 'baby' is the right word."

"No way."

"Yes way." She smiled. Couldn't help it. The words just popped out when she saw Zach go from flirty and cool to frazzled. Nice to know he could lose control with a woman outside the bedroom.

"Have you lost your fucking mind?"

"That's quite a temper." She made a note on her pad. "Guess we'll have to work on that, too. There's probably an anger management class we can put you in."

"If you think this is bad, wait two seconds."

"Okay, do I look like I've lost my mind?"

"No, but you don't look insane either, and right now I'm thinking you might be."

Time to step back and try again. "Look, Zach—"

"I'm the executive chef."

So much for trying a new angle. She answered his bluntness with equal bluntness. "I'm well aware of your title and culinary certifications."

"Does Alex know about this stupid plan of yours?" That handsome smile and all those perfectly aligned white teeth disappeared for good.

"The Board hired me—"

He nodded. "So, that's a 'no' about Alex."

"I don't need his permission, but, yes, Alex knows. The entire management staff knows." And they all supported her. Well, sort of. Zach had many friends, both male and female, so her task was not going to be easy.

"Jenna, you are not in charge of my kitchen, and you know it. About yesterday—"

She rushed to correct him. "This isn't just about yesterday."

"Is it about the new pastry chef, then? Because you came on board right after I fired the old guy and hired the new one. I tried to tell you that after you sent that memo telling me not to make any moves without checking with you."

"So, you do read my memos."

"I had someone help me with the big words."

"You read it, yelled and called me a corporate hack. Some would suggest that type of behavior calls for anger management training, which is now on my list, by the way."

"Some would suggest your timing was bad."

"Is there ever a good time with you?"

"Yeah, any time other than right before the dinner rush would be a start."

She refused to replay this conversation. "Until we get this figured out, all employee matters must go through me. Your ability to make decisions is temporarily revoked."

"That's ridiculous."

"I know you think so, but there is the little matter of the lawsuit. The restaurant's former pastry chef was more than qualified. He had a contract, and you terminated him. He's a bit upset."

"I'd do it again in a second." He leaned back and folded his arms across his chest. "But, really, is this about the pastry chef or because of what you walked in on yesterday?"

"Back to that, are we?"

"I can explain that."

"There's nothing to explain, Zach. I have eyes." The damn image was burned on her brain.

"You jumped to conclusions."

"I walked in and you had a waitress flat on her back on your desk. End of story. It didn't take a genius to work out what was happening."

"Okay, I didn't intend to explain the actual hand positions I was using, but—"

She handed him the envelope she had tucked in her clipboard. "I've made a list for you."

"You're big on lists." He took the paper but didn't look at it.

"These are goals. We're going to work on helping you meet these goals."

He laughed at her. Actually threw back that gorgeous head of silky hair and laughed. When she didn't join him, he sobered. "Good Lord, you're serious."

"Always." She skimmed her copy of the list. "In addition to the pastry chef incident, you've repeatedly broken hotel policy by sleeping with your underlings."

"Underling? They teach you that word in business school?"

She ignored the crack. "One week a waitress. Another week a hotel guest. It's all very unseemly."

"I didn't have sex with a guest. Never."

"That's not what she said."

He jumped off the desk and hovered over her, all six-foot-one standing so close she could smell the light musk of his aftershave. "She's angry because I wouldn't have sex with her, Jenna. If I'd been with her, she wouldn't be complaining. Trust me."

"I can make you one of those little blue ribbons if you'd like."

"I'd settle for some credit."

"We can talk about credits, demerits and everything else when we go over this list."

"You're wasting my time." He threw the envelope on the table and pushed past her. "I have to get to the wedding menu."

"Zach!"

With his hand on the doorknob, he turned back around to face her. "What now?"

"I'm serious."

"You're always serious."

"That's not true." Okay, it was, but he didn't know her well enough to draw that conclusion.

"You know, Jenna. You might want to think about what really has you so angry."

Great, now they were playing word puzzles. "Meaning?"

"Is this really about me sleeping with *other* women?" He threw open the door and walked out.

"We're not done here."

"So you keep saying," he called over his shoulder.

# Chapter Three

Zach walked into the quiet kitchen. After a beat of silence the chatter resumed.

So much for privacy.

"Not like you to yell." Sam, his sous-chef and friend, pointed out the obvious.

"Be glad I stopped with yelling."

"What did dragon lady want this time?"

"Don't call her that," Zach muttered under his breath as he grabbed up his chef's knife and resumed chopping. If he kept this up, the basil would be a pile of green mush. Thanks to Jenna and her long legs and mammoth case of stubbornness, his concentration was shot for the rest of the evening.

"Did you notice she's been spending a lot of time in the kitchen lately?" Sam asked.

Yeah, and he'd stupidly thought that meant something, like she was interested. Now he knew she hung around to collect evidence, take her little notes and come up with some stupid plan to bore him to death. "Hadn't noticed."

"She's a bit bunched in the shorts for my taste." Sam leaned with his back against the counter facing Zach. "The sexy little skirt was a nice touch, though."

"Stop looking at her skirt." Only he had the right to do that.

Sam whistled. "You going to tell me what's wrong with you?"

*Thwak, thwak, thwak*. "Her management style is bossiness. For a lady with an MBA and hotel experience you'd think her people skills wouldn't suck. Or that she'd at least have some."

"Did she try to manage you?"

*Thwak, thwak*. "No."

"Is that the problem?"

"She has some ridiculous idea that she's in charge of setting goals for me."

"What?" Sam stood up straight, all pretense of lazy relaxation gone.

*Thwak, thwak, thwak*. "Like a fucking baby-sitter."

"Does she know she can't do that?" Sam started pacing, then stopped. "She can't do that, right?"

"She thinks she can." Unfortunately, so did he. Maybe he'd taken the playboy image one step too far. It had always worked for him. Kept everyone interested in him and his cooking. Tweaked his stepfather.

It had always worked. Until now. *Thwak, thw—*

"Stop with the cutting and tell me what the hell happened."

"I did. You know what I know."

"Well, does she realize you're the only one in charge of your kitchen?"

Sam wasn't exactly catching on at light speed. Zach wanted to get lost in his work and forget about his stupid conversation with Jenna. Hard to do that when Sam kept harping like an old woman. "Nope."

"Does she know she's overstepping her bounds? She doesn't even work here."

"Nope."

"Does she know what really happened yesterday and with the pastry chef?"

Zach threw the knife in the sink. The clatter of metal on metal rang through the kitchen. "Nope."

"What the hell? Are you going to fill her in or not?"

As soon as he got the chance he'd sit her down and explain that she could practice her outside consulting on someone else. "Nope."

"Damn it, Zach. You think you can answer me with something other than a one-syllable answer?"

"Sure." They both laughed as the tension eased. Zach shook his head in frustration. "Shit, she's a pain in the ass."

"No question. But . . . never mind."

Zach's shoulders tensed again. "What?"

Sam shrugged. "Nothing."

"Not nothing. Something. Spill it."

"She know you have the hots for her?"

"What?"

"Man, Zach, you're smart enough to know you're interested in her, right?"

Zach regretted leading them down this road and slammed on the brakes. "Get back to work."

"That's what I thought." Sam made that annoying whistling sound again. "You're still in denial."

"And you're still not working."

After a few more minutes everyone returned to their stations, and the kitchen hummed once again with activity. Zach contemplated his options, then did what always served him well. He followed his instincts, which meant following Jenna back to her sterile office.

If she wanted a battle, he'd oblige, but they were going to have a little discussion about the source of the real problem between them. Something to do with an instant attraction and an electric zap that knocked him off his feet whenever he saw her. Damn, since the minute he laid eyes on her, all clenched and insecure, he'd wanted her. Only her.

Growing up, the lessons taught to him were about how to use women, not respect them. Despite what Jenna might think of him, he refused to follow that path. He appreciated women. All sizes and all types. He enjoyed the banter, their softness, and the sex.

With Jenna he saw something else. She didn't play hard-to-get. She *was* hard to get. She pretended to be immune to him, and that turned him on. Then there was shy confusion under all that ice. Sure, she had control issues. And, hell, he'd never met a woman more in need of a good—

"Where are you going?" Sam called out to Zach's retreating back.

"To meet the boss."

"Alex?"

"No. The one in the skirt." The one leading him around by the shorts.

He maneuvered his way through a series of monotone doors and endless hallways before stepping into Jenna's outer office. He thought about knocking her door down. The adrenaline pumping through his veins gave him the strength, but he'd rather channel that energy into more productive uses. The kind that involved a little less clothing and a lot more touching.

To get to Jenna's suite he had to get through a puffy wall of Andrea's strong perfume. If he could figure out a way to tell her to go easy on the fragrance and a little larger on the sweater without offending her, he'd do it. She was nice enough. Just had her priorities out of whack.

"Why are you still here at this hour?" he asked.

"The boss insisted. Something about me taking a two hour lunch and owing the office time."

That sounded like Jenna. "She in?"

Andrea shrugged. "She doesn't want to be disturbed."

"She pissed?"

"Always."

Time for some charm. He slid his leg onto the corner of her desk and leaned in close, flashing the biggest smile he could muster. "Maybe you could sneak out now. Go home. See, Jenna and I are in the middle of a conversation."

"Oh." She started nodding. "I get it."

At least one of them did. "Good."

Andrea patted his cheek and sauntered to the door using a walk sure to dislocate a hip on a lesser woman. "If anyone can make Jenna Bartholomew smile, it's you."

As soon as he figured out who the hell Jenna Bartholomew was, he'd get right on that project. For now, he had to concentrate on one Jenna Barrister.

He rapped once on the door, then entered. Better to catch Jenna off guard than with her battle gear up and ready. Good idea, but no one warned him she'd be naked. Not naked, as in totally nude. Naked as in sitting at her desk in her underwear. Naked as in there wasn't enough water in all of Las Vegas to supply the ice-cold shower he was going to need after this.

Gone was the business jacket. She wore only a sleek scrap of white material that hugged her firm breasts and rested tight against her rosy skin. The feminine garment contrasted with the vicious way her finger stabbed at the buttons on the phone.

Probably calling for reinforcements. If Alex was smart, he'd leave the building.

A gurgle of something rumbled up his throat. Now he knew what want tasted like. "Jenna?"

She gasped and lifted her head but didn't move to cover her sexy body. "Zach?"

"We need to talk—"

She found her voice and had no trouble using it. "What are you doing in here? Where is Andrea?"

Still had the full view of her lacy top so his verbal skills threatened to journey back to kindergarten level at any minute. "I sent her home. You're the one I'm here to see."

"You did what?"

He closed the door with a click and walked to Jenna's desk. His dick stirred to life just as his brain waves misfired. How his legs carried him, he'd never know.

She was too busy yelling to notice his weakening control. "Get out!"

"No, and now you know how I felt yesterday."

"I'm not having sex."

Yeah, she really needed to not say the word "sex" in his presence. "Neither was I, but that's a discussion for another day."

"I know what I saw."

"You know what you think you saw."

He tried to concentrate on business, but the frilly underwear thing wasn't making that task easy. He'd always pictured her as the practical underwear type. Really, when he pictured her, she wasn't wearing anything at all. This was one of those times real life beat dreaming.

He nodded in the direction of the phone. "You reach Alex?"

"I don't know what—"

"Yeah, I couldn't get him to take my call either." He dumped his cell phone on her desk. "Let's say we leave Alex out of this and have a conversation. You know, man to woman."

She frowned. "You mean employee to consultant."

Or, naked-lady professional to rock-hard chef. That was how he viewed the scenario. "You can send all the memos you want. Nothing is going to change."

"You'll notice I'm filling out the paperwork necessary to put your employee plan into effect."

This he had to see. In two strides he stood behind her, peering over her slim shoulder and sneaking a peek down her top. He read the papers in front of her.

"What the hell is that?" he asked.

"A performance plan."

The damn thing went on for pages. "How enterprising of you."

"There's nothing wrong with being prepared."

Sam read Jenna right. She needed to unclench. "Unless you intend to alienate half the casino employees, which I wouldn't suggest unless you plan to eat every lunch alone for the rest of your life, the form is overkill."

"The form isn't for everyone. It's for you."

"Aren't I special?"

He turned her chair around, thinking they could talk face-to-face or at least face-to-groin. Shame he didn't plan for the damn thing to spin like a top. With her feet tucked up under her and the seat loose and wobbly, the chair whizzed sideways. He leaned down to put his hands on the back and stop the momentum but pushed too hard.

The damn thing tipped her over backward.

"Shit!"

"Zach!"

With arms outstretched to the ceiling and her slim skirt riding high on her upper thighs, Jenna fell to the floor defenseless. Her mouth formed a tiny "o" as her eyes grew wide with what he hoped amounted to surprise and not fear or pain.

After a slow-motion freefall, the back of the chair bounced against the plush carpet. Jenna's butt slid on what was the back of the seat and landed mostly on the floor with one calf balanced against the armrest and her feet flat against the back of the chair. Her chest rose and fell from the force of her breathing.

She'd never looked more beautiful, all out of control and wild, with her hair mussed and her body sprawled and open. The combination of the fall and the amazing view cost him the rest of his equilibrium. He teetered for a second, then fell right on top of her.

She grunted. He groaned. All in all, not his usual business meeting.

The fall ended with his head wedged between her soft breasts and his upper body flush against hers. The position was a little piece of heaven. His bottom half certainly thought so and swelled in welcome.

"What exactly was that supposed to be?" She choked out the question.

Too much to hope she'd be so wowed by his masterful skill to be upset about the tumble. "That didn't go as planned."

"What, did you plan to throw me out the window and missed?"

He balanced his upper body on his elbows and stared down into her sweet, round face and huge eyes. The dark blue contrasted with her light brown hair. He brushed random strands off her cheek, lingering to feel the silky smoothness of her straight, shoulder-length hair. Damn, she was stunning with a sleek athletic body and lush curves that plumped in all the right places.

As the seconds ticked by his body reacted to all that softness beneath him. He wanted her. Nothing new there. He'd wanted her since he first saw her, but the icy boss-woman reserve held him back.

"You think this is part of an elaborate plan to get in your panties?" he asked.

Her cheeks flushed, but he didn't think the heat rose from embarrassment. She was as interested as he was.

"If so, you need a better plan." She lifted her hands to his chest but didn't push him away.

"This seems to be working to me."

"Uh-huh. Could you hand me my clipboard?"

The woman was as romantic as a piece of toast. "You need me to diagram this for you? I'd rather tell you. Give you long descriptions of what I'm thinking."

"I need to add this to the list of issues we need to address."

"This?"

"The big come-on. It's a tad predictable, I hate to tell you. But, it's easy to resolve."

"You're talking about that stupid list."

"Of course." She flexed her fingers against his chest. "Are you getting up?"

Most definitely. "Excuse me?"

"You know what I mean."

He managed to be both comfortable and uncomfortable. The bottom of the seat jammed into his knee, an armrest dug into his side and his position smothered his erection. And, he wasn't going anywhere. Not when he finally had Jenna exactly where he wanted her. Underneath him.

Finding women had never been a problem, but none of them had staying power. None lingered in his head long after the orgasms ended. All knew the score and welcomed the chance to be a conquest of the playboy chef. He hated the title, but it served its purpose and helped establish the image he wanted to project.

Then Jenna crossed his path, and for reasons he couldn't explain, the playboy moniker no longer fit so comfortably.

"This is a good time for us to talk," he suggested.

"We can talk when I'm sitting down and you're on the other side of the desk."

She still hadn't pushed him away. One sign of discomfort or anger and he'd do the chivalrous thing and jump to his feet. Until then, he'd torture his mind while his body sank against hers.

He snuggled in tighter, fitting his erection in the notch between her legs. "We're having a communication issue."

"You're our only problem as far as I can tell. You and your complete disregard for the rules."

"Shhhh." He brushed the back of his hand under her chin and wondered how skin could get that soft.

"That's going on the list."

"Should I spell it for you? Wouldn't want you to describe the wrong thing."

"I'll be lucky to get out of here in a year at this rate."

Listening to her just ticked him off. Better not to let her stray off topic. "We'll get to your precious list in a second. Let me get this out first—"

She rested her head against the floor. "Go ahead. Get it over with. Give me your line so I can shoot you down and we can move on."

He talked right over her. "You watch people, report and then leave. I keep my kitchen in line."

"I'm not going anywhere."

"Right. Not until we work this out. See, your version of the chain of command around here is—damn!" His chest burned from where she pinched him. "What the hell was that for?"

"To get your attention."

"Christ, woman. If you wanted me to get up, you should have just said so." He pushed up on his elbows and lifted his lower body away from hers.

"I believe I did."

"You know what you need?"

"To stand up?" She actually sounded bored.

Which only made him act more childish. "What I had in mind didn't include standing. Well, not usually."

Something about her brought out the elemental caveman

in him. He'd never be this forward or obvious. He thrived on being cool. With Jenna he acted like a teenage boy with his first condom.

"I'll pass."

"Let me change your mind."

"Are you actually suggesting that after one kiss from you I'll turn to mush?"

He sure as hell hoped so. "Scared?"

"Hardly." She reached up behind him. "I can't reach my clipboard. Can you move a little to the side so I can grab it?"

She acted uninterested, but the longer he stayed there, the deeper the flush in her cheeks turned. The heavier her breathing got.

Yeah, the woman was interested. She just didn't want to be. Tough. He didn't either. But the ignore-each-other's-presence thing wasn't working.

Neither was the not-kissing thing. He leaned down and brushed his nose against her chin, along the other side of her chin, to the deep groove at the base of her neck.

When his tongue flicked out to taste her, her breath hitched in her throat. "Zach—"

He rained kisses across her collarbone. "Just give me a chance."

"I—"

"Shhh." He heard a whizzing sound and a bump but ignored it all. Firefighters would have to drag him out of there. Until then, he wasn't moving.

Jenna had other ideas. "Uh, Zach?"

"Yeah, baby." He kissed up and down her long neck, nibbling her sweet skin.

"What's going on?" She pushed against his chest.

"I can give you a play-by-play, but I'd rather show you."

"Not that." She shoved harder.

"What's wrong now . . ." He opened his eyes to a mostly

dark room. Light seeped in from the opening in the curtains.

Her hands dropped to the floor beside her head, and she started mumbling something about her clipboard and notes. And his lack of control.

"Can I have my clipboard now?" she asked.

"What the hell happened to the power?"

"Well, big boy, either your kissing blew out the lights or something else happened. I'm going with the latter."

He decided to go with the first option. "Damn, I'm good."

# Chapter Four

Yeah, he was good. Damn good. It was kind of hard to prove a point about his lack of control when hers was crumbling faster than his.

What started as a brilliant idea, as a way to prove he couldn't resist any woman who gave him even the slightest encouragement, had turned into a forbidden touch fest. One look, one smile from him, and she turned to mush. She wasn't the mush-turning type. Except with him.

He was exactly wrong for her.

Instead of a push, she rammed the heels of her hands into his chest. "Time to get up."

He didn't even flinch. "Why?"

*Why?* Did his brainpower shut off along with the electricity? "Because we need to see what's going on, that's why."

"Nothing to see. The lights are off. I don't hear the air-conditioning, so I'm guessing we blew a circuit breaker or something."

"You're trying to say your kisses were so good that we blew a fuse? Try again, stud."

His chuckle rumbled against her chest. He flicked back the edge of the curtain and let the light from the Strip stream into the room. "Probably from the construction. Though think how impressive the kiss thing would be."

Dumb didn't begin to describe how she felt at the moment. She'd made every professional misstep imaginable. Lose control? Check. Let her desires overwhelm her good sense? Check. Let her consulting client go one step too far on the floor of her office? That was new, but still a check.

Damn hormones.

What she needed was a little decorum. Getting off the floor and out from under him would be a good start. "Okay, fun time is over."

"Most people would look at the lights being out as a message."

He felt so right there with her body curved into his. "Right. The message being to get up."

He frowned at her and managed to look adorable doing it. "I was thinking more like the opposite conclusion."

She tried to concentrate on his argument, lame as it was, but his firm body kept dragging her attention away. From the impressive bulge pressing against her thigh to his hard-as-granite everything else, she wanted him.

His pretty-boy face and easy charm had attracted her from the beginning. With every day that passed she wanted him more.

"Shouldn't you get back to your kitchen?" she asked.

"Sam has it under control. He's my second in command. He could run his own kitchen and is totally qualified to take over in my absence."

Common sense didn't seem to be working, but she tried again. "Yeah, well, we should be out there checking on the guests."

"Unless you plan to hand out flashlights, I'm not sure what you could do."

"I could . . ." Something.

"We can't do any work. We're all alone. It's dark. I'm on top of you."

"I notice you're not getting up," she muttered under her breath.

"Think of the darkness as the universe's sign we should keep on doing what we're doing." His hand rested on her breast and showed no sign of moving, so it wasn't hard to figure out what the "what" was.

"We need to go," she insisted.

"Most people wouldn't view the lights going out as a reason to stop having fun."

Then it hit her. She was having sex with Zach. On her floor. In her office. She'd even touched his ass. So much for professionalism. Nothing prepared her for Zach.

"Zach, I'm serious." More like embarrassed, but he didn't need to know that.

He lowered his head until his forehead touched her breasts. The move sent an ache spinning from her chest to the damp space between her thighs.

"You're actually going to do it," he mumbled into the thin material separating them.

Her breath caught in her throat. "Do what?"

He skimmed his finger under the edge of her camisole and flimsy bra and outlined her nipple until it puckered. "Call a halt. Go right to the edge and pull back."

"I didn't—" She gasped when he slipped the two layers of silk down, exposing her breast.

Then he palmed her, his hand warm against her chilled skin. "Man, you're beautiful."

She couldn't speak.

"I wanted time to do this." He licked her nipple, flicking his tongue across the tight bud.

She tried to remember her name. Bartholomew something . . .

"And this." He placed his hot mouth over the tip and suckled her. Twirling his tongue over her and wetting her skin.

Someone moaned. She feared it came from deep inside of her.

"So pretty." His reverent whisper tickled against her breast.

Two more seconds and her skirt would be over her head. "Stop!"

"You still want that clipboard?"

"Yeah, so I can beat you with it."

"Well, honey, I'm not usually into that, but I'm game."

She couldn't handle his cuteness. Not now. She needed him angry. Pissed. Whatever it took to get him off of her.

"Your performance plan is getting longer by the second."

She could still feel his lips on her skin. Smell the masculine scent of his shampoo. Taste him. But this was about control. She had to control the situation. Control him.

"I say we work on a different kind of performance plan."

"I knew you couldn't resist a woman, any woman. Here I am taking away all of your authority, and you can't even stay away from me. From a woman you hate."

"I don't hate you."

Wrong answer. "You should."

The rhythmic kneading against her skin dragged her attention from the practical conversation until she had to struggle to listen.

He smiled. "Thanks for informing me."

"I *am* in charge of fixing you."

"You really need to stop saying that. I promise you. Everything on this body is in working order." He exhaled, blowing a warm breath across her exposed nipple until she shivered.

"Nothing has changed. I'm here with one job. You." She'd said it but didn't believe it. Everything had changed. She'd wanted him before. Now the need to have him inside of her—a part of her—swamped her.

"Give me a break, Jenna," he scolded, but his voice stayed soft and gentle. "You let down your guard. Now you're panicked."

Panic didn't cover it. Terrified was more like it. His presence and her reaction to him threatened to ruin everything she'd worked so hard to attain. "I'm concerned about just how much work we have ahead of us."

"You're a by-the-book gal. Let's just add one more sin to my list; then we'll fix that, too."

His thumb flicked over her nipple. She had to bite the inside of her cheek to keep from moaning. "We already have enough work for a year."

The corner of his mouth edged up, erasing his frown and replacing it with a sly smile. "I'll make a deal with you."

Why did she suspect his deals required nudity? "You'll get up. Now."

"If I prove to you for whatever time the lights are off that I can control my base instincts, that I can resist your significant female charms, you drop the fight over the pastry chef. You have to admit I had the authority to fire the dumbass, back off and let me run my kitchen as I see fit."

"Or, you could get up."

He lifted the edge of her bra and camisole and covered her bare breast. "You set the rules. You succeed in seducing me, then I lose."

"Sounds like a warped male fantasy. Only a guy would think having a woman throw herself at him is a viable game."

"True, but it's just between us." He laid his warm palm against her stomach and moved it in tiny circles. "You think

I can't control myself. I can, even with a woman as sexy as you."

Hours alone with her greatest temptation. Hard to imagine a worse career move. "No way."

"Afraid you'll find out I have more willpower than you can tolerate?"

"You'd sleep with anything with breasts, and you know it."

"Well, we both know you have lovely breasts."

"Zach—"

"And, you're wrong. I have standards. Pretty high ones, actually."

"That's wonderful for you."

"You want to test me, then really test me. Put me through the paces while the lights are off and see if my control falls apart."

"This is ridiculous." Then why did it start to sound so intriguing? And, why did the pressure of his hand against her body feel so good.

"Two adults in the dark. You do whatever you want, and my job is to hold you off. You're beautiful and sexy, so any attempt to hold you off will be tough. If I manage it, it will be a testament to my strength of will."

Appealing to her ego was a good call, but she had to be firm. "This is nothing but a way to feed your self-esteem."

His hand stilled. "You think my self-esteem needs feeding?"

"Good point."

"We could scratch one of those pesky problems off your list."

"He has a name, you know."

He nodded. "Matt."

"What?"

This time he shook his head. "His name is Matt." Her

moral indignation would have been more effective if she actually remembered the guy's name.

"You're talking about playing a game with a human being's life."

"He's already fired. This is about you leaving me alone about it. It's also about working out this attraction that's been brewing between us. Let's get it out of the way and move on."

So tempting. Just like him. Delicious and forbidden.

His deep voice intruded on her fantasies. "Make me lose control and I won't complain about losing control over my kitchen."

"You like to complain."

"And I'm damn good at it, so this is quite an offer."

"Do you really expect me to fall for this juvenile fantasy?"

"Oh, it's my fantasy. I've wanted you from the first day I saw you. That's why I win if you beg me."

He wanted her? *Her?* The guy who could have any woman, and did, wanted straight-laced her? "What did you say?"

"You heard me."

"You want—"

"Yes." He whispered the word against her lips.

"How much cooking wine did you drink today?" There was no way she could hold her own against him. She could barely keep up with the conversation.

"Don't need wine with you around."

"This is the dumbest thing I've ever heard."

The corner of his mouth kicked up in a smile. "I've come up with dumber."

"I believe that."

"So, do we have a deal?" He nuzzled his nose against her chin.

"Zach . . ." When he kissed her, her remaining brain cells skipped out for vacation, leaving her hormones in charge.

He flashed that little-boy smile. "The choice is yours, Jenna. The choice has always been yours."

# Chapter Five

"Yes."

Well, damn. She said yes. He was acting like an ass and probably deserved a slap across the face. Instead, she was giving him everything he'd dreamed about since he met her.

He was the biggest idiot in Vegas. That was saying something because Vegas happened to be the vacation destination of many a drunken idiot. "Yes?"

She trailed a finger across his lips, and he opened his mouth to let her inside. "Yes, Zach. As in, I plan to have you on your knees and begging me to make love with you within the next half hour."

"I can last longer than a half hour."

"Really? I actually was spotting you fifteen minutes. One condition."

"Anything." And he meant that.

"What happens in this room stays in this room."

He smiled. "Honey, this is Las Vegas. The land of secrets."

"And this is a big one." She pushed him, and he pushed back with a challenge.

He knew enough about the casino emergency plan to know the generator should kick in and start supplying power to the nonessential areas of the property after about fifteen minutes. The office would be one of the last parts of the complex to get a shot of power, but he could resist her for a short period of time and still have his way on his staff issue. He could let her touch him and kiss him without unleashing his desire.

The more he thought about it, the less sense it made. What seemed like a good plan, a good way to make her admit their mutual attraction and cede control, didn't look like a sure thing now. He knew he should call this off. Walk away.

And he would have done just that, he assured himself, if he hadn't wanted to see just how far she would go. If he didn't think he could have her begging him and forgetting all about the dumb bet before her half hour deadline passed.

"Ready?" Her voice slipped down an octave. The sultry sound thundered through his head in a direct line to his groin.

"You sure you understand the terms?" She couldn't possibly understand his proposal.

"I get it, Zach." She kissed his throat while her hands lifted the T-shirt the rest of the way off his shoulders and onto the floor. "I get a chance to show you my control and demonstrate your lack of it."

"That's not exactly right."

She went to work on muddling his brain. "I get to be on top."

She had predicted he would be on his knees in thirty minutes. He started to think it was more like ten.

"You want me to get up?" he asked.

"Why, Zach, is that a new challenge?" She brushed her knuckles across the front of his jeans.

Maybe eight minutes.

"I don't plan to make this easy." He wondered if those were the last words he'd be able to utter without drooling all over himself.

She smiled, her full lips curled in a satisfied grin. "I'll do all the work. Your job is to relax and enjoy. Then lose."

Six minutes. Maybe five.

"Actually, my job is to fend you off. So, I'll be standing up now," he said.

Every cell in his body screamed in revolt as he lifted away from her and jumped to his feet. He made the mistake of looking down. She stayed on the floor, her slim skirt hiked up and exposing the tops of her black thigh-high stockings.

Then there was her flushed face and puffy pink lips, the outline of her nipples against her silky top. The way her soft brown hair fanned out around her head, just as he had imagined it would look on his pillow.

He started mentally reading off the ingredients needed for his famed crab bisque.

"You don't want to stay on the floor with me?" She slid her feet toward her ass until her knees were in the air and her light blue panties peeked out.

He concentrated on everything but Jenna. The recipe called for crab. There was something about heavy cream or was it Gatorade . . . ?

"Zach? You still with me, honey?" She parted those creamy thighs even farther.

His erection twitched. "You don't play fair."

"Who says I'm playing?" She swung her feet over the arm of the chair and stood up. "The floor has more possibilities, but if you like your women standing up, I'll oblige. My preference is a nice flat surface, all cool and smooth against my back. You know, for traction."

"I'd rather sit."

He picked the chair up off the floor and almost threw it

through the window for fresh air. Instead, he set it back behind her desk and plopped down into it. She couldn't tease his erection if she couldn't find it.

"Good thing I have this nice big desk."

He figured she got the big-ass piece of furniture as an obnoxious symbol of power. Never occurred to him it would work as a makeshift bed.

Maybe he should have stayed on the floor.

"You look so serious, Zach. I don't think you're listening to me."

Shit, was she pouting? "Nope."

"Nope?"

"Right." If he kept his responses to simple one-word answers, he'd be fine. Really, how long could the lights be off anyway? The generator would kick on soon, and he could end this with that ice-cold bath. Or twelve.

She walked behind him. Not seeing her was almost worse than touching her. Almost. After a few seconds, she rested her hands on his shoulders. He could smell her floral perfume as she leaned in close and nibbled on the back of his neck.

"You are an amazing man."

Amazingly stupid. "Uh-huh."

"Smart and funny." The path of kisses wandered across his upper back and landed on his earlobe. "Sexy as sin."

"Sin." He repeated the word without thinking.

She bit down on his skin, then blew hot air across the injury. He held on to the armrests to keep from grabbing on to her.

"You know what I think?"

That he was ten seconds from cracking? Because that was true. "No."

"I think you want me." She walked around the chair and stood just inside his peripheral vision. He stared ahead and refused to look at her. If he did, capitulation would follow minutes behind.

"Yeah." The word strangled out of him.

"Want to touch me. Kiss me." She bent down and whispered against his sensitized ear. "Plunge deep inside me over and over again."

"Christ." His nails dug into the expensive leather.

"Should I show you?"

"No." He'd never wanted to say yes so much in his life.

"Let's just get a little closer."

"I'm fine here." Except for the impending heart attack.

She caressed his chest muscles; then her hand moved lower. "I'd like to sit down with you."

He shoved the chair as close to the desk as possible and tucked his legs underneath. The last thing Jenna needed was more room to maneuver. "There's a chair on the other side of the desk."

"I like this one." She pulled her skirt up until all he saw was miles of pastel blue panties.

"Jesus," he muttered under his breath as his grip on the chair slipped.

What recipe was he thinking about again?

"I'm not sure he can help you, Zach."

She was better than any high-class call girl. He'd never paid for sex, never had to, but he'd heard stories. None of them topped this.

"Your lap looks so comfortable." She lifted her thigh over his legs and straddled his lap. "Should I sit on you or the desk?"

"The floor."

In another room.

In another casino.

In another state.

"You look more comfy than the hard floor." She squeezed

her body between the chair and the edge of her desk and settled in. With her knees nestled on either side of his hips, she brought her lower half in direct contact with his erection.

"Who the hell are you?" He asked the question but knew the answer. She was exactly who he thought she'd be. He knew that under all that steely control and bluster burned a passionate woman.

"The woman who is going to bring you to your knees."

He was already there. "Wrong."

"Zach?"

"What?" he barked out, his nerves shot from the seduction.

Her fingers started winding a lazy trail down his chest, over his flat stomach and to his belt. "I want to touch you."

"You are touching me."

"Inside."

He felt his belt loosen. The screech of his zipper filled the quiet room. His head dropped back against the chair as he counted to twenty.

"Damn," he whispered in a half swear, half plea.

"I've been wanting to do this." Her hot mouth pressed against his cheek as her hand slipped past the band of his jockeys and hovered there. "Do you want me to touch you, Zach?"

He refused to answer.

"I think you do." He could hear the smile in her voice.

Without warning her palm covered his swelling shaft. The soft touch scorched him. She was pure sin. When she wrapped her hand around him and squeezed, he tried to move on to the next memorized recipe. Nothing came to his mind.

Her hand moved up and down on him, tightening her grip. Her thumb caressed his tip and tormented him past the point of sanity. Every time she reached the top, he flexed his hips off the chair to urge her to keep going.

"You feel so good," she mumbled against his chest.

He lost it. His hands went from the chair to her shoulders. He tugged her closer, trapping her hand between their bodies and covering her open mouth with his.

He didn't hold anything back. He used his tongue and his lips. With one hand, he pushed her lower body tight against him while the other raked through her hair, holding her head steady for his kisses. Whispering sexy promises about stripping her clothes off and coming inside her, he gave in to his need.

For weeks she had filled his thoughts. He wanted her. Wanted to know her. To break that firm resolve and show her how good they could be. For the only time in his life, he thanked the electric company for whatever happened to give them time alone without any distractions or reasons to hold back. Every maneuver he'd made up until today failed. This was his chance to be with her.

"Zach?" She sounded as breathless as he felt.

"Yeah, baby?" He pushed her skirt up to her hips and reached for her underwear. He dipped his hands into her panties and squeezed the smooth skin of her backside. While his fingers toured her firm body, his mouth moved to her sweet neck.

"Do you want me?"

"I'm about to have you."

She put her hands over his and stopped him from stripping her. "Zach?"

"Huh?"

She pulled back and stared down at him. "You just lost."

"What?"

"Let's get back to my list."

# Chapter Six

The dropped jaw and stunned look on his face could only be described as priceless. With an ego and self-assurance the size of the entire United States, Zach expected to win. To woo her. To break down her defenses. To have her back out of the deal due to his skills.

He'd succeeded in all but the last, and that one was hanging by a thread. But he didn't need to know that.

Hell, she doubted her legs would carry her if she even tried to stand up. He'd drained every ounce of strength from her and a good portion of her willpower.

She'd never done anything like this in her professional life. Hell, there was nothing professional about her actions during the last twenty minutes.

But this was personal, and she had to get over it. The only way to do that was to stop Zach in his tracks. To hit him where he hurt—right in his sense of maleness. Because if he kept trying, she was going to fold. She wanted, no needed, him that badly.

"So." She took advantage of his surprise to move his hands from her ass to his lap. "Where should we start. I'm thinking we need an apology to the pastry chef. Do you want to tell him or should I?"

"Tell who what?"

Getting hard made him stupid. How cute. "The pastry chef. I won, remember?"

"How do you figure that?"

And that fast, her satisfaction vanished. "We had a deal."

He waited until she let go of his hands, then settled his palms back on her hips. "Still do."

"Wrong. You lost. Deal over."

A smile tugged at the corner of his mouth. "What makes you think you won?"

When his hands started to inch up to the undersides of her breasts, she covered his hands with hers. They'd had just about enough touching. Any more and she'd be back on the floor with her legs wide open and her hands all over him.

"Oh, I don't know, Zach. The fact your dick is hanging out of your pants, your tongue was halfway down my throat and you said you wanted to have sex with me gave me a hint."

"Listen to you. It's kind of sexy when you talk about that."

"It's hard to concentrate when you're sitting there like that."

He glanced down at his lap. "Look at that. Guess things got a little hot."

A little? His love life must be more impressive than she thought.

"You lost." She said it again, thinking repetition might help.

"Am I inside you?"

Every intelligent argument flew out of her head, leaving behind a blank slate. "Excuse me?"

"I can repeat the question, but it's not going to change. You understand what I said."

"You can't honestly think—"

"That the deal was sex? Yeah, I do." He tried to tug her closer.

She leaned back, keeping her weight off his lower body. No need for more temptation. "No, it wasn't."

"Am I on my knees?"

"You're about to be on your ass."

He chuckled. "Apparently, I'm not the only one with a temper issue. Maybe we could take that anger management class together."

"You're cheating." The idea shocked her. She laid a lot of sins at his door but hadn't expected dishonesty.

"I don't cheat," he insisted.

She wanted to believe that. "You don't remember the rules, then."

"Just playing the game. My role was to resist you, remember?" His hands started moving again.

"Stop that."

"Why?"

"How can you sit there and look so innocent? You know you lost. Admit it."

"Never gonna happen."

"Then I guess we're at an impasse."

"I wouldn't say that."

With every second that ticked by, she lost ground. She could feel her resistance waver. "What would you propose, stud?"

"No plans to propose. But, I bet I can have you hot and moaning within the next fifteen minutes."

"No more bets." Not that one. She'd lose that one. A wise woman would avoid bets that included touching or kissing or anything else that would land her on her back.

"Think of it as a double or nothing deal," he said.

"No. Get me the clipboard."

"Screw the clipboard."

"We need to get back to the plan."

"Wrong. We need to get back to this." His hands settled just below her breasts. "The rules are clear this time. You beg and I win. Hell, you beg and we both win."

He leaned forward and trailed a line of soft kisses across her collarbone. With each press of his lips against her skin, her control slipped.

She had sacrificed everything for her career. What had it gotten her? Months on the road without a home or any stability. Never mind the fact she hadn't had sex in over a year and great sex in, well, it had been a long time.

"I said no." She meant yes. Hell, yes.

"One more kiss, then I'll stop." His lips traveled up her neck to her waiting mouth.

"Zach?"

"Just one more, honey."

The words came out as a question, not a statement. He was asking permission, and she wasn't going to deny him. What could one kiss hurt when she was getting what she needed and what she wanted?

"Only one?"

"Yes."

At this point, she'd bargain with the devil to keep him from stopping. "One."

"One," he repeated right before his lips covered hers.

The kiss started light and soft, his mouth touching against hers while his tongue licked her lips. With each sweep he pressed harder, his breath tickling her nose and his lips lingering and learning. The rhythmic dance continued until the voice in her head shouted for more.

"Harder," she said into his mouth.

His fingers spread wide on her back as he pulled her tight against his chest. His kiss deepened, wrapping her in a seductive spell. Their mouths slanted over each other, coaxing and inviting. The touch started a revving in her chest and a dampness building between her thighs. Her heartbeat echoed in her ears as she fought the urge to crawl inside him.

Just as she heated up, he pulled back and rested his forehead against hers. The sudden stop left her feeling disoriented.

"Why did you stop?" *Why the hell did he stop?*

"One." He cleared his throat, but the rasp in his voice didn't leave. "You said one, damn it."

She could barely hear him over the whoosh of her labored breathing. "One."

"Your rule."

He would pick this instance to listen to her. Time for her to take back the lead. "It's not over."

She pushed him against the back of the chair and wrapped her arms around his neck. The chair wobbled, but he somehow shifted his weight to keep them upright. The consideration should have impressed her. It didn't. Rolling around on the floor with him sounded too inviting.

She kissed the side of his mouth. "This is all the same kiss."

"Right."

"All one kiss." She forced the words out between long, drugging kisses.

"Yeah . . ."

When his mouth met hers again, she gave in. From her feet to her head, she surrendered. Need washed through her until every fiber, every cell and every last part of her relaxed into him.

Through the haze, she felt her body float and a sudden lightness fill her chest. She realized he was standing up and taking her with him. With his hands on her backside, he lifted her and rose without ever breaking contact with her mouth or breaking a sweat.

Heat radiated off of him. She could feel his warmth, feel the tension humming over his stiff shoulders and hard back.

She wrapped her legs around his waist to keep him close. There was no turning back now. She would have him, his strength and charm. For at least a short time he would be only hers, and she refused to regret it.

He sat her down on the edge of the desk and tried to lift his head to say something. She wouldn't allow it. She continued kissing him, her need turning into a deep, thumping craving. The closeness and passion, having found it she wasn't losing it now.

His hands caressed her face. The muscles in her stomach turned to liquid, and she fell back against the desk. He followed her down until she lay across the hard surface blanketed by his body.

Balanced on his elbows, he lifted his head and stared down at her. His eyes searching hers for something, she just didn't know what.

His finger traced her puffy lips. "You are so beautiful."

The words were reverent and sweet. She didn't want the words. She wanted to feel, to throw off the professional suit and be a woman.

"Same kiss," she said.

"Same kiss, baby." One hand snaked down her belly and started yanking her silk top out of her skirt.

She reached down and helped him pull. The camisole slipped over her head, his mouth kissing every inch of bare skin revealed by the slow striptease.

"Everywhere," he said. "I'm going to kiss you everywhere."

"God, yes."

He kissed and licked her breasts, tempting her nipples into small, tight buds. His wet mouth sparked life into her sensitive skin.

She moaned as her fingers tunneled through his soft hair. "Zach."

"Tell me, baby. Tell me what you want." He palmed her with one hand as his lips and tongue continued their gentle torment on her other breast.

"You."

When he lifted his head, her skin continued to tingle, each nerve ending awake and alive. A wave of panic hit her when he lifted his body off hers.

"Where are you going?" For a moment she worried he was going to turn on her and announce he'd won the bet, then beat his chest in triumph.

"Not far." He stood by her feet.

"Zach?"

Then she felt it. The gentle grip of his hands around her ankles followed by the slow slide of his fingers up her calves. The tips brushed against her skin, lighting a fire along the nerve endings in his path. When he reached the lacy top of her stockings something flipped over in her stomach.

With an open hand on each thigh, he pushed up her skirt, bunching it at her waist and exposing her panties to his view. She had chosen her high-cut aqua pair. They were her most expensive and sexiest underwear, see-through and light as tissue.

She wore them for him. The idea made sense now, but it hadn't this morning.

Hands slid beneath her, pampering her backside with sweet caresses. When he peeled the silky material down her thighs and over her knees, he moved with a slowness that stole her breath.

He tucked her panties in his pocket. Breaking eye contact, he let his gaze wander over her body. She fidgeted under the close scrutiny. Not out of shyness. Out of need.

"Zach, I—"

He treated her to another lingering kiss before he stepped

back. This time she didn't worry. This part wasn't a game or a way to win an advantage. This was something else, and they both sensed it.

She waited for him to undress or climb up on the desk with her. He didn't do either. He sat down in the desk chair. With his hands against the back of her calves, he scooted her body down until her T-strap shoes rested on the armrests and her butt hovered on the very edge of the desk.

The position left her open to his heated gaze and waiting mouth. Her most private part displayed just inches from his face as if she were a feast. A fissure of wariness wound its way to her brain.

Instinctively, she closed her thighs, blocking his view. "Zach?"

He kissed one knee then the other. "Trust me."

She heard his whispered plea. Couldn't see his face or measure his reaction, just heard his husky voice.

"Zach, why don't we—"

"Lean back, baby. Let me taste you."

This was too much too soon. Too personal. They should start eye to eye. That was within her comfort zone.

"Zach—"

Her voice broke off when his hands eased into the crease between her legs and gently set them wide apart. She thought about protesting until she saw his head lower and felt his tongue lick against her.

His mouth covered her, sucking and suckling, in a steady beat that forced her hips off the desk. Her head turned from side to side as waves of pleasure battered her. She grabbed his hair and begged for release.

Fingers parted her first, then eased deep inside. One, then another, pushed up, then opened as if preparing her body for him. Without a signal from her brain, her lower body rocked and bucked. With each pass of his tongue, each plunge of his fingers, her body tensed and coiled. On one last push, the tension burst, and a grinding moan escaped her lips.

A climax ripped through her. Her eyes closed as the warm sensation washed over her, relaxing her body and returning her hips to the desk.

"Damn." His curse carried a bit of awe.

"Yeah, damn." She opened one eye to peek up at him. That mischievous-boy smile lit his face, but the heated look in his eyes was all man. "You're amazing."

"It was all you. Your confidence is sexy as hell."

She watched him, measuring him from bare muscled chest to his jeans. The fly hung open, and his impressive erection stood out against the black material. "I'm not the only sexy one."

"Why, Ms. Barrister, are you propositioning me?"

"Are you just figuring that out?" She lifted her arms until her hands lay, palms up, on either side of her head.

His hands moved to his pants. In two seconds, he shed the underwear and jeans and stood before her. Every part of him appealed to her physically. His broad shoulders and trim waist. His thick erection and sweet smile.

She opened her legs even farther, letting her knees fall out to the sides. The action drew his attention back to her lower body. His nostrils actually flared at the sight of her open sprawl.

He grabbed up a condom from his wallet and ripped the packet open with his teeth. "This time fast. Next time—"

"Faster."

"I like your style."

His hands returned, this time to bend her legs and push her knees back toward her shoulders. The position opened her to his mercy.

Stepping between her raised thighs, he fit his body against hers and pushed, thrusting deep and hard with one swift move. Their foreplay eased his way. Her body, slick and wet, allowed for just enough friction. Despite his considerable size, he fit perfectly, her body closing around his like a glove, tight and hard.

He thrust in and out, his rhythm picking up speed as his chest rested against her legs. With every plunge, her body clamped down tight, as if her internal muscles didn't want to release him for even a second. The steady beat of his body moving over her, inside her, forced her neck back. A groan spiraled from deep in her chest.

The pushing and pulling sent her body spinning a second time. That tension gripped her again, building and pounding until one final thrust sent her crashing into a second orgasm.

She shouted his name as his body clenched and exploded. With a shudder, his orgasm followed right after hers. She collapsed against the desk. He collapsed against her.

Breathing heavily with hot air brushing her ear, his body relaxed into hers. The considerable weight felt so good and right against her.

She had traded control for passion, common sense for fun. She didn't have any regrets, but now what? They couldn't exactly go back to circling each other and fighting off their mutual attraction.

And what was the proper protocol for "fixing" a guy who seemed just perfect when he was still inside her?

# Chapter Seven

He enjoyed the quiet companionship. No arguments. Just a semidark room with only the sound of their breathing to break the silence. He knew they could be like this, at peace and satisfied.

They lay snuggled on the desk with the smell of sex still lingering in the air. Her on her back with him leaning over her, balanced on one elbow. Earlier she'd shivered, probably more from the aftermath of their lovemaking than an actual chill, and he'd draped his T-shirt across her body.

From his position, he could see her sexy-as-shit shoes, those fuck-me stockings and the damp, dark curls below. She'd covered her breasts with his shirt, but every other inch of her stayed visible and on display.

He absently traced a pattern across her collarbone with his thumb. Her skin was so soft and kissable, as if she bathed in . . . whatever made a woman's skin soft and kissable.

She broke the silence. "Tell me why you fired the pastry chef."

Jenna's inability to turn off her work life and enjoy the moment was a problem. He didn't want to think or work. He just wanted to enjoy her.

"Not the cuddle type, are you? I thought all women enjoyed the cuddling part of the program."

"Neither one of us is the cuddling type."

Apparently they had moved on to the talking part of the program. He exhaled to show his disappointment. "You mean Matt."

"Huh?"

She had a lot to learn about being in Human Resources. "The pastry chef. His name is Matt."

"I know."

"Uh-huh. What's his last name?"

She snorted. "I barely know your last name."

"That's flattering."

She clutched the shirt to her breasts and turned to face him. "Feel free to answer my question."

He debated ignoring the question by mentioning their bet but decided against it. Getting her riled and pissed wasn't what he wanted. He wanted calm. He hadn't experienced much calm in his life.

The crafted image of a carefree playboy served his underlying purpose. To prove his worth separate from that of his philandering politician stepfather, on his own terms and on a career path promised to annoy the old man. After all, only sissies and pussies cooked, or so he said.

Achieving fame in a world his stepfather viewed as too girlie, all while earning a reputation as a charming playboy with principles, was a blow the man couldn't handle. They hadn't talked at all in the four years since his mother died. Jealousy was a bitch.

"You can't ignore me." Her nails bit into his chest.

That was true. He dropped a quick kiss on the rosy tip of her breast. "The fact you're naked makes that tough."

"We've established that I have your attention, so talk."

He shouldn't have to justify. She should accept his decision. But, he could tell from the determined look on her face that wasn't one of his options.

"He stepped out of line. Way out of line," he said.

"Messed up a pasta sauce, did he?"

"Not quite."

"A salad?" She laughed.

Since there wasn't anything funny about Matt's actions he stopped the questions. "More like he hit a female member of the staff."

"What?" She practically screamed the word.

"Yeah, that was my reaction, too." That and a punch to the jaw.

She was sputtering. She sat up, holding his shirt against her breasts. Her furious glare burned down into him. "That man should be out on his ass."

He folded his arms behind his head. "He is."

"Not that way."

"I thought we just agreed I did the right thing."

"On the end result, yes. Not the process. You should have developed a record."

That actually made some sense. "I wanted him out and didn't really care about the paperwork."

"With the proper paperwork, as you call it, we could have fired him and left a trail to follow him wherever he tried to go. Now we have to deal with a lawsuit."

"A frivolous one."

"Frivolous or not, it still counts."

He shrugged.

"That's it?" she asked. "You don't have any excuse?"

"Don't need one."

"You're not a one-man wrecking crew, though you're doing a fine impression of one."

He had his reasons. "If you stop talking for two seconds, I'll explain the entire story."

"Go ahead."

"Matt worked in my kitchen and the waitress is my friend."

She stiffened. "What waitress?"

He'd opened the door to this conversation. Now he was stuck. More explanations he didn't want to give. "I believe you know her as the woman under me on my desk yesterday, but her real name is Anika."

"Matt hit your girlfriend?"

He rushed to correct that mistake. "Anika isn't my girlfriend."

She frowned at him with the stern look usually reserved for high school teachers. "What would you call her, then? Your desk sex buddy?"

"No."

Her mouth fell open. "Oh, shit. Is this what you do? Have sex with coworkers on desks?"

"Of course not."

"Don't tell me I fell for your setup." She started mumbling to herself. "How could I be this stupid?"

"Believe it or not, I didn't knock out the electricity in the entire hotel just so I could have sex with you." Although he might have if he thought about it.

"I'm an idiot." She scrambled to get off the desk. "Show's over. Time for me to leave."

No way was he going to let that happen. He grabbed on to her elbow and pulled her back down beside him. With her legs trapped between his and his chest pinning her to the flat surface, he tried to explain. "You could try listening."

"You could try moving."

"First—"

"I knew we should have stuck to the list." She kept up her mumbling.

He talked right over her, refusing to have one more conversation about her damn list of Zach improvements. "I did not have sex with Anika on my desk. I've never had sex on my desk."

"So—"

"And before you ask, this is the first time I've ever had sex on yours."

"You're trying to tell me you never slept with Anika?"

He debated telling one of those lies he hated so much. As far as he could tell, honesty was a bitch. "I didn't say that exactly."

"Charming. Get off me."

"I've never pretended to be a virgin."

"There's a big difference between virgin and lothario."

He suddenly hated the reputation he'd carefully crafted all those years ago. "I enjoy women, Jenna. I've never lied about that." Or anything else, a fact he was regretting at the moment. "I've been with some but not nearly as many as my reputation suggests. Hell, if I'd slept with all those women, I'd never have time to cook or do anything else."

"But you did have sex with her."

"We're getting off track." He grabbed her wrists and pinned them over her head. "Back to Matt."

When she didn't struggle, he continued. "Anika came on to me."

"Apparently, all women in the hotel suffer from that affliction."

"You including yourself in that group?"

"I didn't exactly fight you off, idiot that I am."

And he was more thankful about that than he could say. "Anika's behavior was nothing more than misplaced gratitude for when I helped her out with Matt."

She smirked. "I could make a joke."

"Don't." He pressed a hand against her midsection, half

to hold her down and half just to touch her. "She was interested but not for the reasons you think."

"By the way you were crawling all over her, I'd guess you were, too."

"No. My history with Anika is long over."

She snorted.

"Jealous?" he asked, hoping that was true.

"Yeah, I can barely see straight. So, is there more to this story?"

Since she clamped her mouth shut, probably to keep from biting him, he filled in the rest of the story. "She kissed me and you walked in. I went after you—"

"—you did?"

"A few weeks before Anika and I were talking—just talking. Matt walked in, got the wrong idea and hit her. She hid all of it, but one of her friends told me. I fired him."

"Bastard."

He hoped she was talking about Matt. "Right. What you saw yesterday was Anika's misguided belief that she owed me for helping her. She didn't. I fired Matt because he deserved it, not because I thought I could get Anika to give me something in return. End of story."

There was more, like how Matt dropped to the floor when Zach hit him. Both times. But, that wasn't all that relevant to the discussion.

"Are you still sleeping with Anika?"

Women never ceased to amaze him. How someone as stunning as Jenna could get all wrapped up in the wrong facts always surprised him. "I wouldn't be with you if I were sleeping with anyone else."

"You said you were sleeping with her."

"Slept. Past tense."

"The way you were touching her looked present tense."

"I would have gotten up. Eventually. The male brain works a bit slower on these issues. Once I realized her intent, I knew I had to stop her." And, besides that, he wasn't interested in Anika. Since he'd met Jenna no other woman interested him the way she did. But, hell, he was a guy and Anika was young and blond and hot. Sure, for a second or two he thought about it. About how easy it would be to find sexual release with someone who knew the score. Who needed him.

Then Jenna stepped into his office, like watching his dreams step into physical form, and the internal debate ended. He wanted Jenna. Only Jenna. Anika felt gratitude. With Jenna he felt anything but gracious.

"I see."

What the hell did she see? "That's why Matt is out."

"He's fired. You're right."

The tension left his shoulders. He didn't even know he'd stiffened until he felt his muscles relax. "Good. Now that we've straightened that out."

He dipped his head and nibbled on her neck. He had one more condom before they had to switch rooms and stock up on supplies.

"So, why not tell me all of this from the beginning? Why not explain to Alex? Why all the secrecy?"

"Why should I?"

"Because you're part of the team. Because you don't run this place by yourself. When we met and I expressed my concerns about the situation, you ignored me."

"I ignored your memo on the issue, not you."

"You know what I'm saying."

"Jenna, look, I do things my way."

She shook her head. "You can't do it, can you?"

"What?"

"Let your guard down."

Trapped. He exhaled, then tried to explain. "This place is small, Jenna. Everyone talks about everyone else."

"And everyone is talking about you."

"Right. As it should be."

"Zach." She said his name as a warning.

"They're talking about you, too. About your plans to shoot to the top of your career by stepping on me."

She shoved against his chest, and this time he backed off. She stood next to her desk. With her hair loose and wild, her cheeks flushed and her hands on her hips, she looked ready for battle. Shame he was the target. The naked target.

"Tell me what you've heard. Who is saying that?"

He shrugged. "Office rumors. That's all."

*Damn it.* The timing of this conversation could not be worse. Just as he was convincing her to loosen up, this caused her to shut down.

"I have a job to do," she said.

"So do I."

"You think I'm using you to get ahead."

"I never believed that." He refused to believe that. The information didn't match with anything else he knew about her.

"But people are saying it."

"I don't care."

A sudden sadness appeared around her eyes. He knew immediately he'd picked the wrong answer.

"Well, I care what people say," she said.

"Jenna, I didn't mean I don't care about you."

She held up her hand, then started picking her clothes up off the floor. "Forget it. Sorry I asked."

"Why are we talking about this?"

"Because you can't turn it off. That Zach-is-King persona of yours never turns off." Undies were back in place, and her skirt was clutched in her fist. "This was a mistake."

"Are we back to square one? I'm the rotten playboy, and you're the ice queen consultant?"

In her state of partial undress she headed for the door. "You're more than a playboy. I get that. But, you don't realize it. You view all women as pieces in some strange public love game. That makes me a plaything, and that I can't tolerate."

She had everything twisted, and he had no idea how to untangle it. With her it was real. Didn't she understand that? "Where are you going?"

"Anywhere you're not."

"Looking like that?"

"Right. Why should I leave? This is my office, so you get out."

He absolutely was not leaving. Once he was on that side of her door, she'd keep him there. "We need to talk."

She walked to the door and opened it. Never mind the fact he was naked and begging, she was kicking him out on his bare ass.

"Jenna—"

Sam stood on the opposite side with a smirk on his lips. "I can come back."

Jenna answered. "No need. Zach was just leaving. I'm done with him."

# Chapter Eight

Jenna shoved her cell phone into her oversized bag and stalked back to her office. The morning had brought electricity and a steady beat of complaints from employees and patrons alike. In the pandemonium, she pitched in to help. Her head throbbed from all of the explaining and apologizing. After walking all over the casino, for what felt like four hundred miles of monotone-colored hallways, she needed to sit down.

It wasn't as if she accomplished anything either. Alex was available to everyone but her. He had either decided to duck her or had been kidnapped and tied up in the bowels of the casino. For his sake, the answer better be the latter option.

She had to go back to her office, check her messages and regroup. She dreaded the return. Her office reminded her of Zach. The desk reminded her of Zach. Hell, breathing reminded her of Zach.

She had expected Zach to be a carefree playboy, but underneath all that shine and flair lurked a decent and grounded guy. Shame he didn't see it or respect her in return.

And he'd touched a nerve. She was looking for another job. Him mentioning the gossip, when he did, like he did, made her feel low. Like a user. With her defenses up, she struck out. Now what?

She pushed open the door to her outer office and saw . . . Zach. Not just Zach. Zach and Andrea. Zach with his hands all over Andrea's purchased breasts.

For a second the world stopped spinning. Everything shifted in and out of focus as a black fury clouded her vision. She went from hurt to fuming in the space of one breath.

Just a few hours after she decided he was out for more than just a good lay, she saw this. His timing made her nauseous. He'd made love to her a few feet away from this very spot just the evening before. The guy didn't even stop to recharge. He ran from one woman to another without looking back or leaving a room.

She knew the rumors. Had heard about his chronic bed hopping, but she had started to see him in a different light. He never lied to her or promised her anything. He protected Anika.

Then he blew it all with this.

"Excuse me." The two words came out in an icy shudder.

Zach and Andrea jumped apart.

"Damn it," Zach cursed when his butt slid off the desk. He added to his profane yell when his arm hit the desk lamp and knocked it to the floor.

Andrea faired better. She pushed back in her chair and made a noise that sounded more like a hiccup than an actual sentence. Despite the surprise, she did manage to fluff her hair.

Too bad she forgot about her clothing. Her tight sweater, today's version being bright blue, hung open showing an ample portion of her cream-colored bra and miles of impressive breasts. Her doctor deserved a medal.

"Ms. Barrister, what are you doing here?"

"This happens to be my office." Jenna tightened her hold on her bag. It was either that or strangle them both.

"I, uh, thought you had a meeting."

Interesting how Andrea knew the part of her schedule that took her out of the office and made her secretary available for a tryst with Zach.

"Your sweater is open," Jenna pointed out in the most disinterested tone she could muster.

Then she turned to Zach. He could at least have had the grace to look guilty. Given her some satisfaction. No. He stood there looking as handsome and self-assured as ever. Fatigue showed around his dark eyes, probably exhaustion from all that skirt chasing, but otherwise he looked great as usual.

She stopped grinding her back teeth together long enough to speak. "Sorry for interrupting. Happy to see you're still using the desk. That's a good prop for you."

"Jenna, that's enough."

"Hardly. If I'd known, I could have stopped for a drink to give you a few extra minutes. You could be smoking a cigarette by now."

Andrea piped in. "Ummm, there's no smoking in here."

Jenna's patience for her secretary's eccentricities was at an all-time low. "It was a joke, Andrea."

"I'm just saying that the smoking ban in the office was one of your first memos. You can't smoke in here now."

"Jenna does like her rules," he said.

"Did you, uh, want something, Ms. Barrister?"

"I want you to button your sweater." Jenna's mind finally started clicking at normal speed. "And since when do you call me Ms. Barrister?"

"Isn't that your name?" Andrea's lips screwed up in confusion.

"Yeah, has been forever, but that hasn't stopped you from calling me Bartholomew."

Andrea shot a desperate glance in Zach's direction. "Well, Zach told me I had it wrong."

Her frustration exploded at Andrea instead of its intended male target. "For heaven's sake, Andrea. I told you my name a hundred times. You didn't need Zach for that."

Andrea shrugged her slim shoulders. "Yeah, but it stuck when Zach said it."

"Of course it did," Jenna muttered under her breath. "One of his many talents, I guess."

Andrea's fingers worked on the tiny buttons until the garment strained across her breasts again. "This is all Zach's fault."

"That's stating the obvious," Jenna said.

Zach tried to break in. "Wait a second—"

"Huh?" Andrea shook her head. "I just meant that Zach told me about my sweater."

For once, she wanted to hear what Andrea had to say. "Explain."

"I need to talk with you." Zach stepped into her line of sight, blocking her view of Andrea.

"I'm talking with Andrea."

Andrea waved her off. "You can talk with Zach. I don't mind."

"How sweet of you," Jenna said.

"You're mad at me. Leave her out of it." His voice sounded so stern and protective.

That realization made Jenna seethe.

"Let me guess. You came to talk with me and fell on top of Andrea by accident." Yeah, that was bitchy, but she was feeling bitchy.

He grabbed on to her elbow and dragged her toward her office.

"Hey!"

"Jenna, I am two seconds away from throwing you over my shoulder and carrying you out of here." His voice shook.

*Anger? What right does he have to be angry?* "Is that the second play in your seduction handbook?"

"This is quite a performance," he grumbled.

"I haven't even gotten started."

"That's what I'm afraid of." He glared at her over his shoulder. "Keep it up and—"

"What? You'll what?"

"I have no fucking idea."

He pulled her into her own damn office as if he owned the place. She guessed that was as far ahead as he planned since he just stood there staring at her. His gaze traveled over her from head to toe, then back up again.

The longer he looked, the more her anger evaporated. A few minutes ago she wanted to poke his eyes out. And, for what? Because he was being Zach Jacobs, super playboy chef. She was acting like a jealous girlfriend. Like someone who cared and had an investment in him.

She didn't. But, she wanted one.

"What now, Zach?"

Good question. All he knew was that he'd needed to get her alone and away from Andrea. Now that he had, his next move eluded him.

He was a guy who always had a next move. Until Jenna. He had no idea how to calm her down or explain. Part of him didn't think he owed her anything. She should trust him. Believe in him when he said nothing happened with Andrea. Hell, Andrea wasn't his type. Any moron could see that. He went for the sexy management type.

He said the first thing that popped into his head. "I didn't make a pass at Andrea."

"Feeling her up is a pass, Zach."

This woman could test the patience of even the most mild-mannered of men, and he wasn't one of those. "Still jumping to conclusions?"

"Still can't keep your hands off the staff?"

She pushed past him and sat down in the chair usually reserved for office guests. Interesting. Maybe the desk and memories of their time in this room pricked at her, too. They made him hard as hell.

He refused to explain and held on to that thought for about a second. Then he did. "She's your staff, not mine."

"True." She crossed her legs. Her ankle rotated in tiny circles.

"And I didn't touch her. I told her one of her buttons was undone, then used the chance to talk about how attractive I thought it was when women wore clothes that were form-fitting but not tight."

That ankle flipped around so fast he was surprised she didn't dislocate it.

"You a fashion expert now as well as a cook?" Her sarcasm level was on high.

And she wasn't budging an inch. He had a few options. He could try to charm her, but her closed stance, with her arms wrapped tight across her chest, suggested she was not a lady open to charm. He could walk out. That one had possibilities, but he refused to back down. Not when making her understand suddenly seemed so important.

Or, he could do what he always did. He could tell her the truth. "We're done talking about Andrea."

"Oh, really?"

"You know I'm telling you the truth. Andrea is attracted to me. I saw an opportunity to help her without being rude, and I took it."

She didn't move, but her eyes softened. The deep blue no longer looked so stormy.

"It is okay for you to want to do well. To succeed. Who cares what the office rumors are? If you want a job, take it. Just don't use me and my career to get it."

The grip around her middle loosened. "That's not relevant to the situation with Andrea."

Too late to stop now. "Be honest about it. Don't come

after me, guns loaded, blaming me for wanting to craft an image that works, when you're doing the same thing."

"I do not sleep around to further my career."

"Neither do I." It felt good to say it. He thrived on honesty, but the one thing he'd never been clear about was the reality of his life. He'd let the public image of him build until it took over who he was and what he wanted. No, he'd never been dishonest, but he hadn't stopped to think about what would happen if he found someone he really wanted to care about and retired his playboy days, both real and imaginary.

"The women, all of it, you're saying it's not real," she said.

"It's embellished."

"Why?"

That was the question. And he knew the answer. "Because I needed it. Like you need the sarcasm and distance your consulting job provides."

"I don't need business advice from you."

"You need it from someone. The bitch goddess thing works, but it has to get lonely."

Her arms dropped to her sides. "Go to hell."

"Right. Don't listen. Keep doing what you're doing."

"I didn't sleep with you to get ahead."

"I. Know. That." He squatted down in front of her. "Neither did I."

"What is that supposed to mean?"

"I made love with a woman who turned my head the first time I saw her. A woman, my equal in every way including on the job, whom I've wanted for a long time. The only woman I've slept with in the last twenty-six days."

"I started twenty-six days ago."

"I know."

"But, you wanted Anika. I saw you on top of her."

"I wanted you, and she came to me and was available, but I didn't take the bait." Not for more than a second, anyway.

When she stayed quiet, he continued. "The first time we met, you walked right into my kitchen and asked to review my menus. The move was so out of line, so superior and wrong, I couldn't help but be interested."

"I was doing my job."

"No, you were doing mine." He caressed her knee.

"This is all about having something you can't have. I wasn't interested, and that turned you on."

He had to concede that point. "Yeah, at first. The idea of attaining the unattainable was pretty damn sexy."

"I knew it." She tried to stand up, but he blocked her way.

"But I'm still here, Jenna. I've had you, and I'm not running or moving to the next business executive or waitress down the hall." He placed a light kiss on her open mouth.

"And?"

"When you figure out what all that means and are ready to talk something other than business, let me know."

# Chapter Nine

"Where is he?"

"Shit!" Sam jumped a foot at the sound of Jenna's sharp voice. The tray of mushroom tarts he was holding bobbled, but he managed to rescue it.

"Nice save."

"My skills are endless." He rested the tray on the counter. "Always nice to see you in the kitchens."

His frown suggested that wasn't quite true. "Now, why don't I think you mean that?"

"Well . . ."

She stepped into the room and let the door swing behind her. A day after the great Berkley blackout crisis, and the kitchen had returned to normal. Everyone wore his or her crisp white kitchen smock. Everyone was busy carting food, cutting food or plating food. Everyone scurrying and active.

Everyone but Zach.

Something squeezed in her chest. "Are you in charge now?"

"I guess."

"Where is he?"

Sam didn't waste time playing dumb. "His mood is worse than yours."

"That's not possible."

And this was the calmer version. She'd stomped around in her office for twenty minutes after she saw the stupid memo from Zach. *He* wrote *her* a memo. The first sentence said something about cleaning out his office. And, yeah, she'd flipped.

Sam looked at her, really looked at her, for the first time. Whatever he saw must have scared him to death because he started talking.

"You okay?"

"No."

"Him either."

The tension eased right out of her. She was surprised Sam couldn't hear the hissing. "Is he still here?"

"In his office. He's packing up—"

"Like hell."

She stalked out of the busy kitchen area with her navy blue sling backs clicking on the tile. For some reason, she'd picked a skirt again today. A slim beige number that stopped right above her knees. The silk blouse underneath matched her dark blue eyes. Bare legs and a sultry perfume rounded out the outfit. Not her usual business uniform but she wanted to feel sexy today.

She tapped on the door as she pushed it open. Zach didn't notice. No, he was too busy throwing books in a box.

"Running away?" she asked in a low voice.

She watched his shoulders tense under his white T-shirt. With aching slowness he turned around to face her. His handsome face didn't show any emotion except exhaustion.

She'd heard he spent the night slaving over the kitchen so that the casino's food service would be back up and running this morning. Every clue pointed to the fact he'd succeeded.

"Cleaning up."

"I see that." She closed the door behind her and clicked the lock.

"Didn't you read my memo?"

"Enough of it to get my butt down here."

"Lucky me." He gathered up a stack of books from the shelf and dropped the armload into the box on the floor.

"I have a question."

His eyes narrowed. "Ask."

"Do you think I used you?"

"No." He didn't flinch. No hesitation. No wavering.

"Did you use me?"

"No."

"Then why me? Of all the female possibilities, why me?" she asked. Her stomach clenched waiting for his answer.

She knew enough about him now to know he wouldn't lie. He'd tell her straight out, even if it hurt. And, if he said the wrong thing, it would hurt like hell because she'd have to leave and not look back.

When he didn't say anything, she tried to end the silence. "If you can't think of an answer—"

"I can, but you should know without me telling."

"I don't."

"Because you're funny and smart. You know your job and all about this hotel. Your motives are pure. You care about people and you're fair. Otherwise, Andrea would have been out on her name-confused ass a week ago."

He never broke eye contact. He read off his list as if he didn't have to think about what to say.

Then he continued as she listened in shocked silence. "You should work here full-time. You deserve a job you love in a place you love. If this is it, go for it. I'll support you a hundred percent."

Whatever she expected from him, this wasn't it. She would have settled for lukewarm praise. Instead, she got a moving speech about all she could be. All she wanted to be but was afraid she couldn't reach. She worried about her motives, that she'd turned into someone who would claw her way to the top, but Zach believed. He made her believe.

"I'm going to succeed at this job and do everything I can to stay on," she said.

"I know."

"I love this casino. The sounds, the vibe, the people. The atmosphere and fantasy, the pure fun and excitement of it all."

"I think it's fair to say the staff doesn't view you as a fun-time gal, but they'll get to know you." The words were sharp, but his tone stayed soft and soothing.

"Everyone assumes stuff about me."

"And?"

"They're wrong. Making this casino thrive and the employees the best in town are my priorities. Building roots and a future is something I want. Something I've never had because my parents were too busy moving me from state to state for their artistic endeavors. I want something of my own."

"Artistic?"

"Actors. And not very good ones."

"That explains the constant moving. It actually explains a lot about you."

That was the easy part. Winning him back could be harder. "I've found everything I need here, Zach."

"That's good to know."

"Everything." Including him. She couldn't let him go. Not now. Probably not ever.

Now she had to convince him.

"Are we agreed you can't hire and fire people without my permission?" She tried to lighten the mood.

"Nope."

"Sam would let me," she said in a flip tone.

He laughed in a sound so rich and deep, her heart flipped over. "No, he wouldn't. I trained Sam. He'd fight you, just like I fight you."

There had been so much between them over the last few

days, and now, just when it looked as if they could settle things between them, he was packing to leave. She needed a grand gesture, and she knew just what to do.

"I came to make a new deal," she said in her lowest, sexiest voice.

His long, lean body froze in position. "I thought you were done with deals."

"I'm through with *your* deals. I set the rules on this one." She slipped her blazer off her shoulders and draped it over the only empty chair in the room.

"Sure you don't want me to sign an agreement of some kind?"

His easygoing charm was in hiding. She intended to bring it out into the open, hoping she still had the power to do so.

"Think of this more as an oral contract."

Heat flared in his dark eyes. "I'm listening."

She walked toward him, dragging her finger along the top of his desk. "You give me five minutes and . . ."

"Yeah?" His hands clenched and unclenched at his sides.

"I'll convince you to stay."

His forehead wrinkled in confusion. "Stay where?"

"At Berkley. At your restaurant."

"What?"

"My goal is to break your control." She stopped right in front of him, her body just inches from his. "I get five minutes to convince you not to leave your job. To stay on here. To give us a chance outside of the office."

She ignored his confusion and moved on with the seduction. Her fingers moved to her blouse. "I'm not the only one with an image problem."

"My image is fine."

"You're a fraud. Acting like a carefree playboy when, underneath all that, you're decent enough to help Andrea without ever taking advantage of her."

"I'm not interested in Andrea."

"That's because you're a one-woman kind of guy." And she was desperate to be that woman.

One by one, she slipped the tiny pearl buttons free and bared her black and navy lace bra. The garment called for stripping. Was made to be seen. It didn't offer an ounce of support, but practical wasn't the point. The point was to entice.

The bulge in his faded jeans proved she'd chosen wisely. "Jenna—"

"My time is ticking away. I only have four minutes left. Hard to imagine what we could do with so little time." The shirt fell to the floor. "Any ideas?"

"One or two."

She reached behind and lowered the zipper to her skirt, then stopped. "Do any of those ideas of yours include me getting naked?"

"All of them do." He leaned back against the bookcase with his fingers wrapped around the edge of two hip-high shelves.

The skirt hit the floor, leaving her standing before him wearing nothing but matching lacy underwear. Underwear that cost more than her electric bill and barely covered her.

The look on his face was worth every penny. The infamous Zach Jacobs speechless and slack-jawed. Who would have thought?

"You know what's going to happen next?" She ran her palms over his broad chest, enjoying the feel of his firm body under her hands.

"Damn, I hope you're going to tell me."

"Even better," she whispered into his ear right before she clamped down on the lobe. "I'm going to show you."

His hands wandered over her bare back, heating her skin in their wake. "Have I ever told you I like your style?"

"Have I ever told you how much I like you?"

His grin disappeared. "Tell me."

Time to risk it all. "A lot."

"So that we understand each other—"

"I want you. Every night and every day."

He just stared, but she'd traveled too far to turn around now. Humiliation hovered just in front of her, but she continued anyway. "When I sit at my desk, you know what I think about? You. I imagine you in the kitchen in those sexy jeans. I remember how you touched me, how you felt inside me."

His eyebrow lifted.

"I want to keeping seeing you. All of you," she said right before she kissed his neck.

He swallowed so hard she saw his Adam's apple bobble. "Jenna—"

"But right now, do you know what I want? You." She lowered his zipper. "Inside me again."

"Damn, Jenna."

"No talking. Just us." She hooked her fingers under the band of her underwear and shimmied out of them, her hips swaying just enough to capture his attention and drag his gaze lower.

When the panties lay on the floor, she wound her arms around his neck. "Well? Do you accept my challenge?"

Instead of answering, he captured her mouth in a searing, soul-searching kiss. It was a kiss of hope with a promise of something beyond that moment.

Her hand traveled down his stomach to his shaft, and he broke off the kiss. "Wait!"

*Wait.* "What's wrong?"

"This." His chest rose and fell from the force of his breathing.

He didn't step back, but she felt the solid wall of refusal he built between them. Everything inside her grew hard and cold. "You're not interested?"

With his eyes closed, he shook his head. "I can't do this."

She wasn't the weepy type, but she was right on the verge of breaking that fundamental rule. "Do you enjoy toying with me?"

"What?" His eyelids flew open, and the intense stare from his brown eyes pierced her. "You're not listening to me."

"You're not saying anything." Except goodbye. She definitely heard something that sounded like the end.

He hugged her tighter. "I want to be honest."

The building waterworks stopped. So did the urge to kick him in the balls. "You're big on honesty."

"Yeah, I am."

"Well, that's just wonderful."

"I'm not leaving," he blurted out.

The conversation was making her crazed. One minute he ran hot and the next cold. Her emotions crested with every word he spoke. "You lost me, Zach. Just say whatever it is you're trying to say."

"I'm packing to move down the hall and into the management wing. That's what was in my memo. The one you obviously didn't read."

"I read a sentence."

"I was asking your permission to move and trying to enlist your help. I thought if I could get you in here, then . . ."

"You said you were packing."

"Yeah, this office."

After a second of silence, a huge grin broke across his face. "Guess I'm not so good at memos, huh?"

"You suck. Stick to cooking."

"Is that an order?"

"I'll send you a memo on the subject."

He nibbled on her shoulder. "I won't read it."

"I thought I had to come here and beg you to stay." The clasp on her bra opened.

"I'd prefer if you begged me to make love to you." His hands found her breasts and started a gentle massage.

The haze cleared from her brain. "You're staying."

"You're not going to ruin the moment and start spouting management bullshit, are you?"

It was her turn to smile. "Can hotel employees date?"

"You're the hotel handbook expert."

"True and, really, some rules were made to be broken."

"And here I thought you weren't listening to me when I said stuff like that."

"So, we're free to date, make love and do whatever else we want."

"I vote yes to all three plus a whole lot more." The nibbling moved to her neck. "But, we'll start with the lovemaking, then go from there."

"You know what this means, don't you?"

He groaned. "I'm afraid to ask."

"You get to cook me breakfast every day."

He gazed down at her, his sweet brown eyes sparkling with mischief. "Baby, I'll make every one of your meals for the rest of your life as long as it means we're together."

"Now, that's a deal."

# TWO OF A KIND

# Chapter One

Caroline Rogers leaned down and did the one, possibly only, act prohibited in all of Las Vegas. She dipped her toes in one of the blue-tiled whirlpool baths in the decadent new spa of the Berkley Hotel and Casino.

The spa sat in the wing connecting the hotel to the new tower currently under construction. When the place opened, Berkley would house the largest and most exclusive facilities for high-end clientele on the Strip.

That was why she was here. To write her travel report about how the good folks staying and working at Berkley coped with the inconvenience. Berkley's patrons weren't exactly known for accepting vacation adversity.

Technically, her alter ego Veronica Hampton would get the credit. Being a hotel critic required anonymity. Her Veronica life provided that.

She'd imagined the visit on the flight here. During every minute of the car ride from the airport. Lounging in a thick terry cloth robe while spa attendants buffed, scrubbed and otherwise pampered her into liquid form. There would be free spritzer drinks and herbal teas. Miles of toiletries to test. Stacks of the hippest magazines to read. All followed by a cleansing shower in a stall with massaging jets aimed at every inch of her tired body.

If her temporary secretary back at the office could read a calendar or schedule a simple job without messing it up, all of that relaxation would have been hers. Instead, she'd arrived a week too early and had to depend on the desperation of an underpaid maid to bribe her way into the closed spa.

She'd put it all in her review. Provide management with a peek into both her view of the spa and the willingness of the staff to bend the rules. Sure, she benefited from the bending, but that did not matter. The rules were the rules. Everything would go in the article.

She tightened the clip holding her long auburn hair on top of her head. Adjusting the knot holding the thick terry cloth towel around her body, she waded into the pool. Therapeutic heat warmed her limbs as the water inched up her calves, then thighs, then brushed against the bottom edge of the towel.

Fragrant steam filled her head as skin turned dewy and warm. Thanks to the scheduling snafu, for the moment all this indulgence belonged to her. She planned to enjoy every last pleasurable second of it. She figured she had a half hour to play before she needed to check out the hotel's hot restaurant for dinner.

She opened the towel and prepared to sink her fatigued body down into the water.

Then a brusque male voice cut through her off-key humming. "What are you doing in here?"

Arms wide open and every imperfect inch of her naked body on display, half standing and half crouching, Caroline froze in place. Her body flushed with heat from head to foot as embarrassment flooded through her.

In a flash she looked at him, saw him staring back at her breasts and snapped the towel closed. Yanking on the edges, she tried to cover as much skin as possible, but every time she tugged from above she showed too much below. Fumbling and pulling until finally doubling over to hide her body from the stranger's view.

"Wow," he said.

The way his gaze wandered down her body and back up again had her stuttering. "I, ummm, what are you doing?"

"You shouldn't be in here," he said, too busy looking at her legs to give her eye contact.

"Can you leave?" So she could wrestle with the suddenly too-small towel in private.

This time he looked at her face with a sappy male grin plastered across his lips. "I'm not going anywhere."

"You can't be in here." Never mind the fact she didn't know where the guy was allowed to be. She just knew where she wanted him, somewhere else.

The man in the expensive navy blue suit, ocean blue tie and matching intense eyes held his hands out in front of him in a calming gesture that was anything but. "I'm not going to hurt you."

She crossed hands, fingers, toes—whatever extra limbs she could think of—over every private body part not covered by the white towel. "As if I'd take your word on that."

His smile turned from sensual to friendly. "We have a misunderstanding."

"Nightmare" was the word he was searching for. "Not if you leave now."

"I won't come any closer but—"

"You're damn right you won't." Yeah, that was better. Anger. A little frustration. A dab of attitude. No panic. She couldn't show fear.

A muscle twitched in his cheek at her turn from fear to pissed, but he didn't say a word.

Smart man. Right now she'd probably drown him if he uttered one stinking word. Amazing what a little adrenaline pumping through the veins could do for an otherwise terrified woman. "Turn around and keep your hands where I can see them."

"Why would I?"

"Because I'm naked."

"I know." That gaze went traveling again.

"Eyes up here." She pointed at her face. "Now, if you'd face the back wall, I'll get myself together and get out of here."

He actually looked as though he had to consider the request. After a delay lasting five seconds longer than forever, or felt like it, he gave her a slow and reassuring nod. "Whatever you want."

The staring didn't stop. He watched her face, but that gaze bounced down to the towel and up again a few times. And no turning around.

"How about you do it now," she said, less as a suggestion than an order.

"Damn. Sorry."

Took forever but he finally turned around and faced the wall, with his hands up. The move didn't help one bit. Her capri pants, aqua sweater and underwear were on the hook off to his right. To get to her clothes she had to go through him, and that just was not going to happen.

"I have a suggestion," he said.

A smooth, warm voice. Probably hid the psyche of a serial killer.

"Shhh." She needed to think. She always worked better with clothes on. That fact wasn't exactly known to her until right this second, but now she knew. The more clothes she had on, the more in control she felt. Good to know.

Despite the warm water lapping against her legs, a shiver ran through her body. She guessed fear and uncertainty were the culprits. Probably explained her puckered nipples, too.

At least she hoped so. Scary situations didn't turn her on.

Whatever people needed, fine, but that wasn't her thing. Though a nice firm butt and broad shoulders like the pair this guy possessed had been known to turn her head. Sometimes all the way around.

"There are—" He spoke up.

"I shushed you."

"Right." She could almost hear the smile in his voice when he said that.

"Stay shushed."

"Yes, ma'am."

"Shhh." This time her voice, or to be more exact, her screech, bounced off the Italian-tiled walls.

He cleared his throat.

"Who are you?" she asked.

Nothing. Not a peep.

"What, now you don't feel like Mr. Chatty?" When he stayed quiet, she tried again.

Still nothing.

"Hello?"

"I thought I'd been shushed." His deep voice boomed through the quiet room and echoed off the walls.

Okay, he had a point. Further proof being naked made her stupid. "You can talk, providing your eyes stay forward."

"Can I put my hands down?"

"No." Not as if she could stop him, but he asked so she answered. "I'm waiting for a name."

"Alex."

A tiny fissure of dread spread through her bones. She knew from her file Alex Mitchell was the assistant manager of Berkley. He was an up-and-comer with a sterling reputation, cute smile and big bank account. Known as your basic no-time-for-anything-but-work guy. She suffered from that malady as well, so she understood his work tendencies.

"Do you have a last name?" she asked.

"Mitchell."

She mentally calculated the probability of someone named Alex Mitchell having access to this part of the hotel and having the guy be an Alex Mitchell other than *the Alex Mitchell*. Yeah, not that likely.

"Your turn," he said.

"No."

He chuckled. "If you let me move five feet to the right, I can get you a robe."

Robes? That would work. Grab the robe, pick up her clothes and run like hell. No way was she struggling into a bra with him standing right there.

"Show me," she said.

"In the cabinet." He hitched his chin in the direction of the sleek wood doors outlining the entrance to the room.

She'd tried that already. "You need a key."

"Good thing I have one, then."

Wasn't he just hysterical all of a sudden. "Okay, but one inch over five feet and I'll . . ."

What? She'd what? Scare him with her cellulite?

"No extra inches. Check. Here I go." He slid, one foot then the other, in an exaggerated style and inch by inch.

"You can move a little faster." Since she was naked and all.

He started to lower his hands.

Unease returned in a flash. "What are you doing with those hands?"

"I don't keep the key in my ear. I need to grab the ring out of my pocket, stick the key in the lock and—"

"No quick moves."

"Slow. Fast," he said in a sing-songy voice. "You need to make up your mind."

She needed to kick him in the ass. The charm thing probably was supposed to put her at ease. And it did. She just wasn't so sure she wanted to relax and let down her guard.

She'd heard rumors about Alex. Many travel professionals credited him with Berkley's smooth running. Part of her job was to stay away from Alex. No management perspectives. No marketing and PR campaign stuff. Just true and honest information gathered from observing regular employees and the clientele.

Not seeing him would have been a shame because he sure looked good. Six-foot-two with the trim body of a runner and the deepest blue eyes she'd ever seen. Throw in the brown, slightly ruffled hair, chiseled chin and high cheekbones and, well, she could see why management had made him the front man.

Heck, at twenty-seven, her biological clock hadn't started ticking yet, but her hormones hit overdrive with one look from this guy.

"How did you get in here?" he asked as he reached for a soft pink robe and three fluffy towels big enough to cover her queen-sized bed at home.

Since she was already lying, why stop now. "The door was unlocked."

He peeked over his shoulder at her. One glance and she clenched the towel even tighter. She wasn't a prude, but her body didn't exactly call for nude sunbathing. She looked better in a towel. In any covering.

"Sorry." He immediately faced the wall again. "Try another explanation."

She didn't really have one. "I walked in."

"Not possible." He held out the items in her general direction but didn't try to look at her.

She eyed the robe and uncurled her body from its defensive position. Water splashed over the side of the pool as she stepped out. She crept around the floor and headed for his outstretched arm. The covert tiptoeing probably wasn't necessary, but she did it anyway.

"Don't you wonder why I'm here?" he asked.

"Sightseeing?" She reached out to grab up the material.

"Sort of. I saw you."

Her hand stopped in midair. "Huh?"

"Actually, security saw you and called me." He shook the robe as if trying to get her to take it.

Freezing to death was the least of her problems at the moment. She turned around in circles with her arms crossed over her breasts and her wet feet slapping against the cold ceramic floor. "You have cameras in the women's spa?"

"Yes."

"That has to be illegal, or it should be."

"It's only for emergencies and heavily regulated. The cameras require a security code for access and will generally be turned off."

"Like when someone watching the monitor feels horny?"

"Sounds like an emergency to me, but it's really about something happening in here and us being unable to get into the room. If that situation would occur, we'd need to be able to see."

She still didn't get it. "When would that happen?"

"We have a two-thousand-page manual that sets out disaster scenarios. Trust me. Anything could happen."

Sounded like a flimsy male excuse to her. "Where are those peeping bastards? How dare they invade my privacy."

She kept looking around, turning and twisting her body at every conceivable angle in search of the blasted cameras.

"Actually"—he cleared his throat—"you're trespassing."

"A technicality."

"More like a misdemeanor." He lowered his arms.

"Hands."

His arms lifted back to shoulder height again. "Rather than send in the security crowd to drag you out of the whirlpool area, I came."

"You are?" As if she didn't know.

"The assistant manager. The person in charge of dragging women out of whirlpools around here."

Her body stopped moving, but her head continued to spin a little. She chalked it up to the warm room and the idea of being the entertainment for groups of men carrying guns. Then she sent up a little prayer that she hadn't done anything embarrassing.

She refused to think about that. "This kind of thing happens often enough that the casino needs a specialist?"

This time he coughed, more than likely to hide his laugh. "Unfortunately, no. The job perks are limited to profit sharing and a 401K."

"So, umm, where's the camera? And since I've asked nicely two times, you need to give me a response." The information was vital to the where-not-to-look-and-where-not-to-flash-her-butt issue.

"Cameras. Plural. They're in the lights. They're off. Give me two minutes to verify."

"How?"

Two fingers disappeared into his pocket. Out came a tiny phone. He flipped open the cover. "Damn."

"What now?"

"I can barely get a connection in here." He pressed a button and started talking. Talking turned to yelling and precise enunciation, as if the person on the other end didn't speak English or couldn't hear. "What do you see?"

If the guy on the other end said anything that sounded like "her big ole ass" or anything close, she'd drag him through the phone and hold his head under water. Her body wasn't obscene or huge, but she weighed about ten—make that fifteen—pounds more than she should. For some reason, all of that extra baggage landed on her lower half.

He snapped the lid shut. "I could barely hear them, but they didn't even know I had gotten in the spa. The cameras are off. They've been threatened with termination if they come on. They're smart enough to know I can check these things."

"I might want to check on that myself."

"Has to do with computers and digital recordings and a bunch of stuff you probably don't want to hear about." He turned around and faced her. "Let's introduce ourselves."

"Turn back—"

"I'm still holding the robe," he pointed out.

"And now you're facing the wrong way." With one hand clenched against the towel, she reached out and grabbed the robe.

"Don't know if I'd agree with that."

Before she could form a snappy response, or even think of one, the lights blinked off. The loss coincided with the exact moment she ran out of brain power.

"What the hell?" Alex echoed her thoughts exactly.

"Did you turn off the lights somehow?" The hotel had everything else. Remote control lighting wasn't a stretch.

"This isn't about someone hitting a switch."

She guessed this was why he was in charge. He seemed to know the important stuff. "No?"

"Everything stopped. I can't hear the whirlpool jets either. I need my phone."

She saw a tiny light in his hands and could see him make another call. "While you're at it, tell them to turn the lights on."

"I'll get right on that," he said.

"Your hotel might get a good rating after all."

"What?"

*Whoops.* "Nothing."

Lucky for her, the other person must have gotten on the line because Alex started yelling and speaking slowly again. "What happened?"

She leaned over his shoulder and got a whiff of his cologne. Smelled like the beach. "What are they saying?"

"Shush."

She pulled back, a little stunned. "Did you just—"

"Shush," he repeated.

He shushed her. Actually told her to "shhh."

A few minutes later, and after quite a bit of swearing and yelling, some of it by Alex and some by her, she heard a little click and watched him hang up.

"Well?"

"Phone's dead."

"Terrific."

"That's not all."

"Whatever it is can't be worse than the group-peeping incident."

"You haven't heard it yet."

She knew she should have spent more time at one of the casino bars and less at the spa. "Tell me."

"A transformer blew."

She exhaled. "Okay. That's not so terrible. Sure, we have to get out of here in the dark. Not fun, but doable."

"The transformer blew in the new building. The one connected to the spa. The alarm and locking system isn't working right."

The conversation took a sharp left turn into please-be-kidding territory. She could feel the bad news waiting to spring on her. "And?"

"We can't get out."

"You better mean out of Vegas."

"Out of the spa."

She blinked. Twice.

"I'm afraid it's just you and me and the whirlpools." He took a step closer to her. "Hope that works for you."

# Chapter Two

"It could be worse." Alex pitched his voice low in his standard everything-will-be-fine management style.

He didn't move. No need to startle her or make her anxious. They would be spending at least a few hours together. Having her cry every minute of that time didn't appeal to him.

Neither did the prospect of getting her all riled up and bossy again.

"Think of this as an adventure," he suggested.

"A cruise is an adventure. Going on safari is an adventure. Being stranded with no air and no electricity isn't my idea of fun and excitement."

"We have air. It's one of those perks we provide along with the room rate."

"You're saying no one ever died in your hotel."

She had him there, but good managers didn't talk about those statistics. "Not of asphyxiation due to poor air-conditioning. We've had our share of disgruntled spouses and a depressed person or two, but nothing caused by the hotel."

"Good thing or that high rating of yours would have suffered."

"Not on my watch." Keeping that perfect rating was his number one goal. The new owners of Berkley were in the process of assessing every aspect of the complex. Paring down the staff and getting rid of nonessential personnel topped the agenda. As the corporate man stationed at the hotel, his was the neck on the chopping block. One wrong step and he'd be busing tables at an all-night place off the Strip. He'd done that work for years.

No. Thank. You.

He'd made his way from trailer park to luxury suite in his thirty-three years of life. Sure, he wouldn't fall all the way back to one meal a day and four shirts in his closet. He was smarter now. Older, more polished and marketable. But even one step backward was unacceptable.

"I can't see my hand," she said.

"Technically that shouldn't affect our rating."

"It's just odd that with all the amenities and extras around here, we can't find one person in this hotel who can break us out."

Sure, when she put it that way it sounded stupid. "Blame technology. It's a new system. We've been working out the bugs."

"The bugs are winning."

"Which is why this wing is closed." Her trespassing status didn't seem to bother her. He'd get the truth on that eventually. They sure as hell had time.

He heard a whooshing sound followed by a soft thud. "What was that?"

"I dropped the towel."

Towels brought him back to her naked body. Great. Now he wouldn't think about anything else.

"The generators are on and supplying emergency electricity to essential locations, like the elevators, the casino, the kitchen and a few other places."

"Hate to tell you, Alex, but food is the least of my concerns."

His eyes started to adjust to the darkness. He could make

out shadows. Soon the room should be in focus again. Until it was, he wasn't moving. No need to take an unexpected plunge into the whirlpools.

"I'll remind you of that comment in about three hours when you're trying to eat the rocks out of the sauna."

"If I try, you have permission to tie me down until the insanity passes."

Tie her down. More visual images. If he were going to fantasize about her—and he was—he should at least know what name he would be shouting out as he came.

"Care to tell me your name?"

More thuds. He tried to remember how many towels he gave her. There seemed to be a lot of dropping going on.

"Caroline." She exhaled with enough drama to knock him over.

"Anyone ever tell you that you're less charming in the dark?"

She snorted. "What makes you think I'm charming in the light?"

"Call it a hunch." From his memory, she looked pretty damn charming without any clothes on. "Last name? Maybe those parents, or a husband, gave you one of those, too."

Yeah, that was subtle. Why not just grab her hand and feel around for a wedding ring?

"Rogers."

The husband question remained open. He dropped the interrogation and looked around. Why he bothered, he didn't know. Not much to see. A person could always find a light on in Las Vegas. Except in this room.

Stuck in a dark room with a gorgeous naked goddess. Yeah, he knew *exactly* how to handle that situation. If he were back in his suite, he'd use a little music, candlelight, a bed. Nothing hard about that agenda. This was a different story.

"Tell me you have some plan to get us out of here." More shuffling, even a scratching noise or two. Her voice came from the same place, so he didn't think she'd moved, but she was mighty busy doing something.

"Believe it or not, Caroline, I don't control Nevada Power."

"How about air?"

"I don't control that either."

"How about you tell me what you do control and we'll work with that."

"Remember what I said about your charm and sunlight?" More shuffling. "What exactly are you doing?" He had to ask since the curiosity was killing him.

"Putting on the robe."

"You're still naked?" Just saying the word filled his head with mental images of her on the side of the pool. Naked. Covered by him.

Two months of job-imposed celibacy caught up with him in a rush. Not long for other people, maybe, but too damn long for him. Exercise could relieve the stress only for a short time. Then he needed another outlet. One with firm breasts and soft skin.

"I had a towel, remember? It's gone now."

Oh, he remembered, so she could stop talking about it anytime. Hell, every cell in his body knew. A man didn't forget something like that. He just figured she threw on the cover somewhere along the line.

If he had known she stood less than five feet away, having a leisurely chat with the voluptuous redhead—soothing her nerves—would have been the last thing on his mind. The first would have been about his clothes hitting the floor.

He knew exactly what her body looked like with and without clothes. He had gotten the call from security and checked out the monitors. At the time, Caroline hadn't stripped down. Fully clothed and bold as could be, all hot and curvy in her slim pants, she walked around the spa taking notes.

When he got to the spa, he expected to find her scribbling on her pad. The plan was simple. Confront her. Get an explanation. Confiscate the journal and kick her out.

Instead, he got nudity and a front row seat to an acrobatic towel routine. Having seen the dressed version while standing at the monitors, he'd imagined the undressed version.

Reality proved much better than guesswork. Miles of curvy pale skin. Red curls above and below. Full, high round breasts. Yeah, all better than any journal he'd ever read.

Earlier, when she had asked him to turn around, he almost thanked her for the excuse. A bulge in his pants the size of Montana could only have gone unnoticed for so long. One look at that and she would have screamed the walls down. Now, in the dark, whatever happened in his pants was his business.

"Are you dressed now?" he asked.

*Please let her be dressed.* Wait . . . what the hell was he thinking?

"I'm wearing the robe, but I'd appreciate it if you would move this along."

"Not sure what it is you think I can do. We're stuck. Can't-get-out-or-break-the-locks stuck."

"Don't you have people for this?"

She was having trouble with the concept of stuck. "Like what, professional burglars? That's more up your alley. Know anyone?"

"A locksmith."

"It's not that easy. Everything runs via computer. Without electricity, we won't have computers. The system will need to recycle, and this, being a supposedly abandoned area, will be the last priority."

"That's very linear of you."

Squinting, he tried to make out the outline of the room. It was so damn dark that his eyes refused to adjust. "Have I pointed out that you weren't supposed to be in here in the first place?"

"About a hundred times."

"The head of security knows where I am. He also knows the paying guests and casino folks come first."

"Who told them something so dumb?"

"Me, and thanks." He moved his foot and brushed against something. He figured the towel had landed on his shoe. Rather than risk being wrong, he stayed put.

"We need to work on your priorities, Alex. You're in charge. You have to get out and help. It's your job."

He agreed on one level. It killed him to be stuck in here when people needed him out there. On another level, he knew the guests would get desperate fast. Faster than the problem could be fixed.

"I'd guess the people stuck in elevators think they should be first. Then we have the people stuck on the top floors without air-conditioning or light. I'm a priority, just not the first. The paying guests are first."

"I'm a paying guest."

She had an answer for everything. "Which room was that again?"

"Fifteen seventeen."

Okay, she came up with the number pretty fast. Maybe that part was true. "Did you also have an appointment here at our closed spa?"

She ignored him. "Can we at least go sit down in the lounge?"

"No."

"You enjoy standing on the hard floor?"

"Believe it or not, I'm not enjoying any part of this." But for some reason he was. Sparring with a woman wasn't something he normally enjoyed. He worked. He ate. He slept. Worked out. Had sex whenever possible. That was about it until his job situation leveled out.

"Why don't we skip to the part where you fill me in on why we're here rather than sitting on the leather couches in the lounge."

"This room has the lock system on it."

"The computer malfunction thing again?" Her voice grew louder. "Afraid someone will break in and steal the herbal tea collection?"

Loud and sarcastic. A terrific combination. "I could argue that someone already did."

"I told you—"

"We have the lock in here because the lawyers told us to. Something about water and additional liability."

"Damn lawyers."

"I was thinking more like, damn Nevada Power."

"The smell from that room over there—"

"The eucalyptus room?"

"That's the one. The odor makes me a little queasy."

"I'll comp your room if you promise not to get sick." Hell, he'd give her whatever money was in his wallet if she made that promise.

"Deal. If it gets too bad, I'll sprawl out on the tile. Anything for a free room."

He had an aha moment. "That's it."

"What's it?"

"Wait right here." The room finally started coming into focus. He just needed to get from one side to the other. Where was a flashlight when a guy needed one?

She snorted. "Where would I go?"

"No idea."

"You're moving around," she said in a loud, clear voice.

"And you're shouting." He dragged his fingers across the wall to guide his way. "Feel free to stop anytime."

Now he knew why the fire marshal refused to sign off on the paperwork to let them open until some corrections were completed. Emergency lighting just moved to the top of his check-on-that list. The lack of windows and heavy darkness spelled liability in big, bold letters.

With slow, steady steps he passed by the steam room and the sauna, gulping in a large swallow of moist, then dry, air. Heat radiated off those doors. The eucalyptus room would be next. The medicated smell filled his nose before he touched the glass.

A few treatment rooms sat on the far side of the eucalyptus room. Those used for bizarre things like mud baths and other crap he couldn't imagine women paying hundreds of dollars an hour to have slathered on them. But they did. All the time.

"Alex?"

"Still here. Didn't break out without you." He saw the door he wanted and felt around the wall for the door handle.

"Care to tell me why you're running laps around the room?"

"I'm walking." He opened the door and stepped inside.

"Is there a point to all this activity?"

"There should be candles in these rooms. Something about setting a mood while women relax in a big vat of mud."

"Sounds heavenly."

"Sounds disgusting. But, if people want to pay big money for it, I'm all for it."

"Not a patron of the spa?"

This room was even darker. He skimmed his palms over the treatment table and over to the countertop and shelves on the opposite wall. "Not something I have time for these days."

"No massages?"

"A guy touching me while I'm lying on a table without clothes on? No thanks."

"What about a female therapist?"

She was smiling. He could tell by the light note that moved into her voice. Good. Last thing he needed was her afraid and worried. "If I'm naked and a woman is touching me, I won't be paying her. Breaks my code."

"You have a code?"

"No paying for sex. Ever."

"Pretty sensible rule, but one that might be tough to abide by in this town."

"Las Vegas is the last place on Earth where a guy needs to buy sex. Like the drinks, you can usually find it for free."

She laughed in a sound so rich and genuine that he stopped feeling around the cabinets for a second.

"Find anything?" she asked.

He shook his head to force out the mental image of her naked and laughing while sitting on the edge of the whirlpool, touching him. No need to go there. He had enough on his mind with the possibility of the promotion or layoff, the rumors of a secret reviewer on the premises and now the blackout. Getting laid was his lowest priority.

Well, it should have been.

Someone needed to tell his dick because it had been stuck at attention since the minute she stepped in the pool and flashed him that hot body.

Caroline wasn't one of those skinny stick-figure types. With full breasts and rounded hips, she didn't qualify as part of the antifood crowd. She'd eat without a mystery trip to the bathroom afterward. Been down that road more than once. No thanks. More female baggage than he needed.

"Found the candles." He grabbed up what he could find.

"Good start."

He waited for her explanation. "Meaning?"

"Unless you plan to eat them, you might want to find something that produces, you know, a flame."

"Damn," he whispered under his breath. "Still looking."

Okay, he forgot. Since all his blood was too busy rushing to his lower half, he had a good excuse for the lack of brain power.

He gathered up the candles and matches and made the trek back to her side. "Still out there?"

"Right here."

"I'm following the sound of your voice." Actually, he didn't need her voice. He sensed exactly where she was. He could even smell the light musky scent of her perfume.

"Want me to sing?"

"Can you?"

"Well, no. But your options are limited. It's me or, that's right, nobody." She started humming a show tune. He'd heard it before but couldn't remember the words.

He retraced his steps and stopped right in front of her. "Need a light?"

She laughed. "Always the clever one, aren't you?"

Her fingers brushed against his, soft and light. The gentle caress sent a signal straight to his dick. Touching her touched off a need inside of him. A need to have her.

"That's why they pay me the big bucks." Standing this close, having her hand rest against his, his professionalism would have flown right out the window if the room had one. "Okay, then. Let's set up the candles."

Her fingertips went from the back of his hand to his handful of candles. "I'll take these."

Her voice deepened as the temperature in the room spiked. He couldn't see her face, so he didn't know if she felt the spark. But the mood shifted. Anxiety eased away. So did the light banter.

A new tension filled the room. A tension he recognized and fought off. Having sex with a guest was out of the question. His superstar chef, Zach Jacobs, suffered from that particular problem and had an outside consultant on his ass as a result. He'd pass on that.

"I—" His damn voice cracked. He cleared his throat and tried again. "Put them in a circle."

He handed her the candles and set her to work on that task. As a soft glow filled the room, he walked over and grabbed up a few more towels and robes. No reason to sit on the hard floor when expensive Berkley products were nearby.

He turned around, his arms filled with his terry cloth booty . . . and stopped. Two towels tumbled out of his grasp and fell to the floor. He tried to move, but his legs refused. All he could do was watch her.

Caroline sat with her legs crossed in front of her in a circle of white light. She combed her lean fingers through the deep auburn curls that fell to her shoulders. A slim gap in the robe highlighted her creamy pale skin. Slim bare feet with toenails painted dark red peeked out at him.

Damn, she was beautiful. Not magazine or celebrity attractive. This beauty came from a different place. Natural and genuine. Uninhibited and classy.

He was a fucking dead man. There was no way he could spend ten minutes with this woman without wanting to plunge deep inside her. But damn.

Screw his code. Screw his job. He wanted her.

She pulled a loose curl toward her mouth and wound it around her finger as she looked up at him. "What are you thinking?"

That if he didn't have her soon, he'd burst. That he was

two seconds away from diving into the cold-water plunge pool in the center of the room. That he'd never had a thing for redheads before, but he sure as hell did right now.

"That I'm sorry you're stuck in here," he said instead.

She frowned and cocked her head to the side. "Really?"

"You don't believe me?"

She dropped her hair and leaned forward, causing that gap to slip open a little more and show more of that lovely skin. "I'm not."

"Not what?"

"Sorry."

Yep. A dead man.

# Chapter Three

There were worse things than being trapped in a room with a gorgeous man. About ten thousand worse things. Make that a million. The problem was being stuck with *this* man. Alex Mitchell.

Her job was to write an undercover exposé on how a top-notch hotel handled a big-time renovation. To do that, Alex was the one man who could not know her real identity. The one man she'd meant to avoid. That proved impossible.

The blinding attraction to him didn't bode well. Caroline could almost see an Alex spotlight sidebar on her review. Management style: above average. Ability to handle stress: outstanding. Kissing: exceptional. Use of hands: could teach a class.

Sure, the last two were a guess but, come on. A guy who looked like that would know how to kiss. How to use his hands. How to make a woman convulse with pleasure. And writhe. She'd never writhed in her life and wanted to give it a try.

"Here." From five feet away the object of her lust thrust out an armful of towels in the general direction of her head.

One could assume from the distance he kept between

them that he didn't want to touch her. Since in this case the "one" was her, she could say that was her exact assumption.

Something had the usually calm management professional scurrying. Maybe he was afraid of fire.

"It's about a hundred degrees in here." And getting warmer by the minute.

"More like two hundred," he said.

"Then, what's with the towels?"

"They're for the hard floor. Without chairs we need something to soften the ground." He dropped the towels. Most landed on her lap. One fell on her head. Not the most debonair move ever recorded, but a nice thought.

His easygoing charm had vanished along with his smile. In a second he'd flipped from sweet to serious. Something bugged him. She just didn't know what.

She dried off her hair and spread out the rest of the towels in a fluffy makeshift bed. Now to end his hovering.

She patted the floor beside her. "Come sit with me."

From the look on his face she would have thought she asked him to perform open heart surgery with his fingers and a paperclip.

"Problem?" He had one, that much was clear. She just had to get him to admit it.

"No."

Uh-huh, as if that answer didn't just shout problem with a capital "P." "The look on your face says yes."

"Other than the loss of electricity and a hotel in chaos?"

"I mean a problem in this room."

"I'll make a deal with you." He hitched up his pants and sat down on the floor across from her. Rather than try to fold his six-foot-two frame into a pretzel, he extended his long legs in front of him in a lazy sprawl.

She tried very hard to concentrate on the conversation

bouncing back and forth between them rather than the flash of electricity that zinged through her when his calf brushed against her bare knee.

"Wanna bet on how fast we get out of here?" she joked.

"I don't gamble."

"You don't—"

"Never."

"Are you sure you understand how Vegas works?"

The left side of his mouth kicked up in a shy smile. "I make it my business to know everything."

Well, crap. Was he saying he knew who she was? Why she was here? "Care to impress me with your knowledge?"

"Think I could?"

Every minute of every single day. "As you said, we have the time."

"I admit, the idea of impressing you sounds, shall we say, interesting." He shifted his legs until his leg rested against hers.

Yep, electricity. Very impressive indeed.

"Go ahead. You have a captive audience."

He chuckled as he loosened his tie. With one shrug, his suit jacket fell from his broad shoulders and landed on the tile behind him.

Him undressed. Her in a robe wearing nothing underneath but heated skin and a rampage of hormones. No, that wasn't going to work.

"What are you doing?" she asked as if the live demonstration wasn't enough of a clue.

"Getting comfortable. If I don't strip down, I'll melt. We have plenty of beverages in the refrigerator, but dehydration is still a possibility."

"You make that sound so sexy."

He froze in the act of unbuttoning his shirtsleeves. "Liquids do it for you, huh?"

"I didn't mean . . ." She stopped because she actually did mean that.

"I can talk sexy if that's your preference."

She shook her head, trying to dismiss her stupid side comment. If only she could wipe the words right out of the air. "Of course not."

"Sure?"

*Of course not.* "Yeah, I'm sure."

"In that case, let me warn you. The plan is to take off my shirt and tie but leave the pants on." He started unbuttoning the shirt.

"Makes sense." In a let's-all-be-adult-about-this way. Only she wasn't feeling very professional or businesslike.

"For now," he added.

"I take it you have another plan for later." She almost hated to ask but did anyway.

"If I start to pass out, the pants come off."

No, no, no. Those pants needed to stay on. "Wouldn't want you to be hot."

"Too late," he muttered under his breath.

"What?"

"Tell me the truth. Someone let you in here." Not a question. A statement.

"Yes."

"Who?"

"Don't know."

He raised an eyebrow but didn't push.

"Honestly," she added.

He pulled the tails of his shirt out of his pants. "You strike me as a woman who can read a name tag."

With all that shifting and moving she caught a flash of flat stomach right above his belt. Her temperature spiked in response. If this kept up, she'd be the one fainting.

"I purposely didn't get a name so that the employee couldn't get in trouble."

"Clever." He slid the shirt off his shoulders and dragged his stark white undershirt along, exposing skin tanned honey wheat and a muscled chest that dipped in a vee to a trim torso.

"Yeah, I'm brilliant," she mumbled. So brilliant she couldn't see a conflict of interest when she fell right over it.

He leaned back on his palms. "Why?"

"Probably had something to do with all that schooling my parents paid for and—"

"Break into the hotel." That amazing smile lit up his face. By candlelight his body glowed, giving him a godlike quality.

"I thought we were talking about how smart I am."

"That's a given."

The compliment made her smile, even if he did include it in a throwaway line. "Want to trade test scores?"

"Don't change the subject." He tried to look serious, but the lightness in his voice gave him away. "Someone sneaks into my spa, I want to know why. Call me controlling."

She could not answer his question without fear of exposing her work as a reviewer and performance appraiser for Hotel and Tourism Inc. Her company assessed and critiqued hotels, then published the results for all to see. Hotel owners and managers hated the process, and with good reason. She couldn't be bought.

To remain neutral and effective, her job demanded confidentiality. She could travel to hotels to perform her work only while undercover. Hence the Veronica persona. No one knew Caroline since that name didn't appear anywhere on the reviews.

"I'm in town on assignment." The assignment being his

hotel, but she left that part out. "Wanted to try out the fancy new spa. When I found out the new space didn't open until next week, I scheduled my own tour."

"For some reason, I believe you." He sat up straight and fingered the edge of the towel next to his knees.

Only a guy could double over and not be self-conscious about rolls of fat folding over his pants. Not that Alex had any fat. But, since she had one, or two, or three, of those not-so-little rolls, she vowed to sit perfectly straight and not breathe out until someone rescued them.

"I guess I have that kind of face."

"Pretty?" he asked with a grin.

Flirting wasn't her style. Business was her style. She engaged in a fling now and then. More then than now, but she knew the score. Business and pleasure didn't mix.

"Honest." She pulled her robe tighter around her waist. "And the flattery is a nice touch."

"Sounds as if you think I'm making a play."

"Are you?" *Please let him be . . .*

"What do you think?"

"You look good. Great even." The words came out before she could shove them back in.

Then there was only silence. Heavy, draining silence.

Nothing moved in the room except his smile which grew wider, if that was even possible. His lean stomach dipped in a little, as if he inhaled a sharp breath.

"Thanks." His soft voice, so rich and deep, pulled at her.

"You're welcome." Not the sexiest comeback she'd ever come up with, but at least she was able to say something. With her tongue stuck to the roof of her mouth, anything other than babbling drool seemed like a step in the right direction.

The more he stared, his blue-eyed gaze steady, the more

sweat rolled down her back. The soft material of the robe suddenly scraped against her skin.

"Just one more thing," he said.

"Go ahead. I'm sitting down."

"Good, because I need to take off my pants."

# Chapter Four

"Your . . . ?"

Alex decided to fill in the blank. "Pants."

"Did you say . . ."

"Pants. Off." He marveled at his ability to hold a conversation when his insides kept revving up for action.

If the new wide size of Caroline's almond brown eyes was any indication, he'd just slipped down a notch or two on the good-guy scale. Perfect. He didn't want her to think of him that way. Good was for high school crushes. For the male friend who watched chick films with a woman on her dateless Friday night.

No, he didn't want to be the good guy or anything else that meant responsible. He'd spent a lifetime doing the right thing in order to move ahead. Right now he wanted to chuck all that. Forget about his job and the rumors that those damned Hotel and Tourism folks were planning to send someone over.

"Maybe I gave you the wrong impression," she said in a measured way that left a beat of silence between each word.

"You didn't."

"I think we have a miscommunication," she insisted.

"Caroline."

"No, hear me out." She twisted the ends of her belt into a knot.

"I'm listening." Even though the rush of blood through his veins made that tough.

"This is a sexy setting."

"It's an enclosed space filled with pool chemicals."

"Right." She nodded three or four times. "Very sexy."

"Caroline, I think you need to relax."

"Flickering candles—"

"—dwindling air—"

"—the whole nudity thing."

Okay, enough. He wanted her attention. "Caroline."

"We're partially naked. Note, I said partially."

He didn't jump into this part of the conversation. No need to stop her now. Not when she finally hit on a thought he could appreciate.

"There's no reason to take that a step farther at the moment," she continued.

Wrong direction. "Caroline."

"We don't know each other."

"Yet."

"And we're naked—"

"Caroline!"

She cocked her head to the side and frowned at him. "Why are you yelling?"

"Why do you keep saying naked?"

"Huh?"

He exhaled deep and slow in an effort to calm his growing erection. "Look, I'm on fire over here."

Her gaze bounced down to his pants, then back up again. "Oh."

"Yeah, there's that. I can't exactly hide my attraction to you. But that's not what I'm talking about."

"Your what?" It was either the heat or the dark, but something caused that dazed look on her face.

"I'm talking temperature. I'm sweating like crazy over here."

"You're hot?"

Didn't he already say that? "The pants need to come off, but I don't want to scare the hell out of you."

She seemed to visibly collect herself. "Men without pants. Yeah, not my big fear in life."

"Probably depends on the man."

The tension building between them eased with her laugh. "And the pants."

"Let's get back to me." He didn't wait another second. He jumped to his feet and unbuckled his belt.

At first he concentrated on everything but her. It was either that or lose what was left of his control. His lower body didn't follow the rules where Caroline was concerned. One look from her, one peek of creamy skin through that seam in the robe, and his dick kicked into overdrive.

Damn the job and the pressures. He wanted her. On the floor. In the pool. Hell, sprawled out on the sauna benches. The place didn't matter.

"Why did you stop?" she asked, her husky voice cutting through the silence.

With his hands on his fly, he lifted his head and stared at her. "Excuse me?"

"You stopped. You started to unzip, then nothing. You froze. I thought maybe something was wrong."

Now she wanted his pants off. That qualified as progress in his book. "I was thinking."

"About what?"

*Getting that robe off you.* "Nothing in particular."

"If I didn't know better, Alex, I'd say you turned shy."

He scoffed. "Hardly."

"Nothing to hide?"

Just a growing erection. "I was trying to be sensitive."

"To what exactly?"

"You."

"Me? I'm in a robe and naked underneath. Does that help?"

He choked. Big thudding coughs rumbled up from deep in his chest.

"Alex?" She scrambled to her bare feet and stepped up to his side.

"Grhmpf."

"Are you okay?"

He coughed a few more times before straining out a sentence. "Do I sound okay?"

"I can't have you dying on me. I'm not going to die in here alone."

"Charming."

With one hand banging on his back and the other resting on his forearm, she crowded in on him. Her breasts pressed against his side. The soft scent of flowers tickled his nose as her warm skin heated him through her robe.

"Answer me. Are you okay?" Concern laced through her voice.

"Except for the sore back," he grumbled.

"I was helping."

"Define help." He stood back up to full height. Without even trying, he towered over her by about five inches.

She was tall and curvy and fit against him just right. And she hadn't moved. Hadn't stepped away. Still burned him with her touch.

"So, is the drama over?"

"Not quite."

Before she could protest or question, before he could pull back and examine his motives, he leaned down and traced his lips over her cheek. Her smooth skin warmed under his lips. With butterfly kisses, he learned her face. Inhaled her unique smell.

"Alex?" Her fingers closed around his arm.

"I'm going to kiss you."

"Oh." She nibbled on her bottom lip.

"I was hoping for something more than that."

"How 'bout, this is stupid?"

"Not that." His kisses traveled to her earlobe.

"Dangerous?"

"Definitely." Then across her chin.

"A little naughty?"

"I sure as hell hope so."

When she shifted her head, he took full advantage and trailed his lips down her neck. "Forbidden."

He pulled back and stared down into her worried gaze. "No. I've wanted to do this forever."

"We've only known each other for less than an hour," she whispered.

In one sweep, he captured her lips in a deep, thundering kiss that pounded through every inch of him. From his head to his groin, he felt her. Not just in the way her body pressed into his, sinking in until her terry cloth robe rubbed against his bare skin, but in the way she filled his head.

Her hands slipped up his chest to loop around his neck. Fingers plunged through his hair. She didn't wait for him to take the lead. No, she threw herself into the kiss. A warm, wet mouth slanting over his. An eager tongue dipping deep between his lips. His body on fire.

He wrapped his arms around her, pulling her body tight against his. Skin touched robe from hip to chest. Her full breasts crushed against his hard muscles. His erection pressed against the junction of her thighs.

With each sweep of her hands, each caress over his shoulders and neck, his erection grew. Blood thumped inside him. His body tensed and hardened. The desire he felt for her grew.

The warmth of the room settled over their bodies. Eucalyptus filled the air. He could feel steam. He knew the sensation wasn't real, but he felt it all the same. As if humidity and heat mixed with the air, making it heavy.

He broke the kiss but not the contact. He couldn't let her go. He needed to see her pale skin again.

With a gentle touch, he slid the robe off her shoulder, exposing a firm, round breast. His lips wandered across the slope of her collarbone, then traveled down to the fleshy top of her breast to the very tip.

As his mouth settled over her nipple, his fingers slipped beneath the other side of the cloth and teased and caressed her hot skin. Her breast fit in his palm as if he had been born to touch her.

"Caroline." He whispered her name against her skin. Kissing her very tip, then blowing on the wet area. With each pass of his tongue, her midsection bucked.

"Yes, Alex." She grabbed the back of his head and pulled him closer.

Kissing, touching. All of it worked for him.

He needed his pants off and her robe on the floor. Their bodies lying on the stack of towels. Their inhibitions forgotten if only for a few hours.

When he reached for his zipper her hands were already there. Pulling back, he placed his hands over hers and stopped her from lowering the tab. "We need to slow down before I explode."

A haze caught her in its grasp. She kissed her way over his shoulders to his biceps as her hand cupped his length through his pants. He tried to laugh at her enthusiasm, but the sound strangled in his throat. The feel of her hand over his erection made his eyes cross. Made a churning sensation spiral up his body from his feet to his brain.

"There won't be a later if you keep doing that," he pointed out.

He kissed her again with a mixture of hope and promise. The need to grab her, take her, nearly overwhelmed him.

But he stopped. He wanted, no needed, to be gentle. To make her understand that this was not how he operated. That she wasn't just an available body.

"Alex?"

"Yes, baby." He broke the kiss and went to work on the knot on her robe.

"You still have your pants on."

"Give me five seconds." His fingers pulled and tugged.

She caressed his face with her palm, then stopped. That's when the pushing began. "Wait, Alex. We have a problem."

"No, no wait." Hell no. That wasn't the answer.

Anxiety replaced excitement in her eyes. "You're right."

"You don't happen to have any scissors, do you?"

Her hands closed over his. "About the waiting."

He stopped fiddling and looked at her. Her full mouth had that puffy, fresh-from-sex look. The flush on her cheeks continued down to her chest.

And she was calling a halt to the sex. She didn't have to say it. He could see it in her crooked smile and shiny brown eyes.

"Damn it, Caroline. Don't start listening to me now."

"You're on fire." Her fingertips soothed over the back of his hand.

Finally, she understood. "Exactly. That's what I've been saying." He tried to kiss her again, but she ducked to the side. That had to be a bad sign.

"No, your skin." This time she touched his forehead like a nurse, not a lover.

"Caroline, you have had sex before, right?"

"Of course." She kept taking his temperature with her hand.

"You know what happens to a man's body when he's aroused."

"I paid attention in fifth grade health class, if that's what you're asking."

The whole scene bordered on embarrassing. Here he was making a move and plotting a heavy bout of sex, and she was trying to find him two aspirin and a thermometer. Yep, nothing manly about this scene.

"Alex, listen to me. You're thinking about sex, but this room is getting hotter by the second. You need to take off the rest of your clothes."

"That's what I was trying to do."

"We both do. But not for sex."

# Chapter Five

From the gleam in Alex's eye, Caroline guessed he still wasn't getting her point. She tried again. "We need to cool off, not heat up."

"You're still having trouble with priorities."

"Like living?"

"Now who's being dramatic."

He acted as if he were the only disappointed person in the room. She craved his lovemaking. Wanted to know his touch. Feel him push deep inside her.

But one of them had to think with a smidgen of logic. Now that she was, she wondered how she'd lost so much control over the situation. Making love to Alex would be a mistake. The epic kind. The career-ending kind. Without her job there was no her.

She'd spent so much of her life focusing, traveling and finding a job that would allow her the freedom she craved. Freedom from her religiously suffocating youth. From strict rules and a small town in Utah where no one ever questioned a parent's right to cloister kids in church for hours each day.

No, she couldn't tempt it. Being with Alex would be a different kind of freeing, but one that could lead to the end of everything. The conflict of interest couldn't be ignored.

Then there was the problem with his body temperature. The one locked on dangerously high. He chalked it up to heated lovemaking. She worried debilitating fever was the real cause.

"How about if I take off the pants and we pick up where we left off?" he asked with an eagerness that made her roll her eyes.

"Your perseverance is impressive."

"One of my many skills."

"I bet." She took another step back, leaving him standing in the candlelit circle bare-chested, fly open and black briefs peeking out.

Damn, he was sexy.

"Let me show you one or two of those impressive skills," he suggested.

She wanted nothing more. "Alex, you're not listening."

"Trying not to. See, I'm a healthy guy." He swept a hand down his body.

As if she needed evidence of his fitness . . . "Let's keep it that way."

"I'm fine."

She folded her arms across her chest. "Strip."

That sexy smile played on his lips. "Now you're talking."

"You're going in the pool."

The smile faded as fast as it appeared. "What the hell are you talking about?"

"The whole way under." She glanced over her shoulder. "One of these is a plunge pool, right?"

"I refuse to answer on the grounds that . . ." He made a face.

"Yes?"

"You'll actually listen to me again."

Even disgruntled and surly, he was hot. "Alex, you're going in. By now the water is cool but not cold. Exactly what you need."

"Says the lady who plans to sit on the dry ground."

She ignored the frowning and general male I-don't-wanna attitude. "We need to get your body temperature down."

"Then you shouldn't have let me see you naked."

A warmth crept into her cheeks. "I didn't really have a choice."

"You could have skipped the trespassing and prevented all of this."

"And missed meeting you? Missed seeing you in this charming mood? Say it isn't so." The idea turned her empty stomach. Not meeting him would have been a loss somehow. She didn't analyze it. She just knew it.

She stumbled across a lot of businessmen in her work. Dedicated, smart guys. Alex possessed something more. Wit, looks and charm. The whole package.

"I'll get in on one condition," he said.

"You'll get in condition or not. I am not dealing with a dead guy all evening. Move."

He crossed his arms over his chest. "We need a bargain."

She mimicked his stance. "You need an antibiotic."

"Bargain."

"And a doctor."

"Bargain."

"And possibly a lobotomy."

His eyebrow inched up. "Are you ready to hear my deal?"

"Thought you didn't gamble."

"This is a negotiated settlement, not a bet."

The words rolled off his tongue as if he said them every day. In his business, dealing with complaints and whining, he probably did. "Spoken like one of those lawyers you profess to hate."

"That's what they teach you in law school."

Good grief, this guy had more degrees than she did. "Thought you went to business school."

"Business and law."

"Aren't we the overachiever?"

"How did you know about my business degree?"

Damn. One slip too many. She knew the banter would lead to trouble. She just assumed it would be naked trouble, not reveal trouble.

"I assumed you must since you run this place and don't look very old."

His eyes narrowed. The move was slight, but she picked it up. "Sounds like a lie to me. You seem mighty knowledgeable."

"I'm a smart woman, remember?"

He hesitated a second, then pushed on. "Okay. Ready?"

Relief whooshed through her. "I didn't agree to any settlement."

"You get in, too." He reached for that zipper again.

"That's the fever talking."

"We strip down and both cool off."

Now she felt warm. "Sounds like a typical male solution to me."

"It could be fun as well as medicinal."

That sure sounded sexy. "Hell, no."

She didn't even have to think about it. Getting in a pool, where he could see all her extra inches, never going to happen. "I'm not the one whose brain is slowly being eaten away by fever."

"Thanks for that visual image." He moved in until their forearms touched. "You go in. I go in."

"Ah, the male brain at work."

"The fever hasn't gotten to it yet."

"That's a bit juvenile, don't you think?"

"You won't get me in that water otherwise. And you do seem so determined to save me."

"Maybe not so much anymore." She dropped her arms

to break the tenuous contact between them. "What's wrong with you?"

"I'm frustrated."

"You? I'm the one arguing with a brick wall. A sick and feverish brick wall."

"Wrong type of frustration." He gestured at his pants. "Do you need a powerpoint presentation?"

Nope. The bulge said it all. "Fine. Off with your pants."

"Off with the robe."

A clothing standoff. This was new. Someone had to engage in a little maturity. Looked as if she was the only potential candidate in the room.

Reaching out, she took his hand. Ignoring the tiny sparks jumping between them made the task of rescuing him a bit harder, but someone had to step in before he slithered to the floor from heat exhaustion or whatever else plagued him.

"Come with me."

"It's about damn time," he mumbled under his breath.

She led him twenty feet away to the shadowed part of the room. To the edge of the plunge pool. "This is it, right?"

"No."

The flickering candles cast light on the area but not much. She could see everything well enough to keep from falling down. Not to read.

She relied on memory. "Okay, so the little sign planted in that waterfall rock display that says 'plunge pool' is a lie?"

"Why did you ask if you knew?"

"Why did you lie about it?"

"I thought women expected men to lie."

"Now, there's an attractive theory on women."

"Thanks."

She blew out the breath she'd been holding. "I mean your absolute lack of knowledge when it comes to women."

"Test me." He spread his arms wide. "I'm ready."

"Right after you prove you're not going to pass out or die on me." The words slipped out before she could stop them.

"Agreed. Now that the bargaining is over, want to seal the bargain with a kiss?"

"Get in before I push you."

She tried to retrieve her palm to do just that, but he didn't let go. Instead, he slid his other hand up her forearm and rested his fingers there. The loose grip didn't threaten or bind her. It staked a claim.

Time to concentrate on the rescue. "Doesn't that look refreshing? Four feet of cool water just waiting for your big body to jump right in. Get to it."

"You need to get out more."

"No kidding," she said under her breath.

"Does too much work and not enough play make Caroline a dull girl?"

"I'm not dull." A little driven, yes, but—"Don't change the subject."

He shrugged his shoulders. "Not exactly bold either."

"What?"

He shrugged his shoulder and did a fine impression of a dejected teenage boy. "Just thought you'd have more guts."

Indignation raced through her, followed by a splash of common sense. "Nice try."

"What?"

"Throwing your testosterone around like that. I know what you're doing."

"I don't know what you're talking about." The sparkle in those ocean blue eyes gave him away. Looked innocent but underneath all trouble.

"The secret male-challenge thing isn't going to work with me. You can double-dog dare me and the answer is no. Get in."

He looked down at the water. "The least you can do is sit on the edge and keep me company."

"Where else am I going to go?"

"Eucalyptus room?"

"You want me to be sick?"

"Now, there's something to look forward to."

In slow motion, he pulled the zipper over the bulge in his pants. Every click of metal on metal shot through her. The tab reached the bottom just as he gazed down at her through unruly bangs.

"Was it good for you?" he asked.

"You have no idea." Really, he had no idea. Amazing was more like it.

He dropped the material to the floor. A grab for the band of his boxer briefs came next. The second he started pushing down the last barrier between his body and the air, she jumped to action.

"Wait." The lean-muscled thighs were enough. She didn't need a full striptease. "What do you think you're doing?"

"Obeying your every command."

"I said pants. You can get in the water with your briefs on." The unbelievably sexy briefs that were now resting on his hips and begging to slip lower.

"And come out to wet underwear? No thanks. Been there. Done that."

"You a big camper or something?"

"Never mind." He stripped the briefs off and stood back up, proud as could be.

Why not? Damn, the man defined perfection. No flab. No marks. Just tanned bare skin, muscles everywhere and, yeah, *every* part of him impressive. Long and thick and ready for action.

No way was she disrobing now. Not when he looked like

that and she . . . didn't. Every single one of those extra ten, definitely fifteen, pounds of hers jiggled in response.

"You could have warned me before the show started," she pointed out.

He grinned. "Be careful what you ask for."

"Yeah, well, I learned my lesson." She gathered up the bottom of her robe to midthigh, careful not to flash him the fleshy upper part. "You gonna stand there all day doing the Adonis impersonation?"

"Depends. You impressed yet?"

"I have eyes, don't I?"

"That's good enough for me." With the arguing abandoned, he sat down on the edge of the pool right beside her. Muscles across his shoulders bunched when he lowered his body into the pool.

"How is it?" she asked, not caring one bit about the water.

"Fucking cold."

"Big baby."

"Don't see you getting in." He sat down on the water bench right next to the steps and balanced his arms on the edge of the pool.

"Another challenge?"

"Just complaining."

"Well, never say I'm not a good sport." She dipped her painted toenails in the water and fought off the urge to squeal. Icy cold covered the tip of her foot, convincing her she had already taken the one step too far. The hot air made the water feel colder than it was. Her skin didn't seem to know, but her brain did.

She tensed and clenched her back teeth together. Screaming would mean he won. There would be no yelping or other high-pitched sound coming out of her. No way.

"Feels good, doesn't it?" he asked.

She hoped his smirk would freeze in place. "Very refreshing."

"Kind of like a swim in an icy pond must feel."

He talked snotty, but under the water he rubbed down his arms and thighs. In fact, there was quite a bit of action going on under the water. And she had a front row seat to it all. To watch his erection which, despite the cool splash of reality, stayed switched on ready.

He gazed up at her. Even in the darkness his brilliant eyes sparkled with mischief. "You're still on the first step."

Because her foot had frozen solid to the tile. "Here is good."

He patted the pool edge right next to his head. "Sit here."

"You're supposed to be concentrating on cooling off."

"Feel me."

"Excuse me?"

"My forehead, but if you—"

"Here." She scrambled to sit down, even though that put her butt right next to his mouth. With her feet pulled up underneath her and her robe tucked between her thighs, she touched the back of her hand to his forehead.

"Well, nurse?"

Not her fantasy, but she could play along. "Better. Do you think you're sick?"

"No."

"Just your time of the month, hmmm?"

The universal male look for "ewww" formed on his lips. "No. I've always had trouble regulating my body temperature when it gets really hot. Happens when I run, too."

"So naturally you live in the desert."

"I go where the job takes me and stay in the air-conditioning. Trust me, there are worse things to this job than the heat."

"Such as?"

"Trespassing guests."

"Very funny." She let her hand fall to his shoulder. Heat radiated off his skin, but the frying sensation had disappeared. "I'm serious. What's so bad about working here?"

"Difficult guests with unreasonable expectations and requests. Questionable management styles. This new construction project."

Questions bombarded her brain. She wanted to grab up her notebook and get down quotes for her review. That was all she wanted.

Well, not all. For the first time, gathering information wasn't her only interest. She wanted to know about him, too. To form a connection and see where it led.

The realization hit her out of nowhere. The idea was so foreign and odd. Ties weren't her thing. She avoided anything that would hold her down. Something about Alex made her wonder if her rules should be broken.

"For instance," he continued, "no one asked the people who do the hands-on work around here about the proposed layout of the spa."

She switched back into worker-bee mode. "Not even you?"

"Most were ignored."

"Like?"

"There is a balcony off the men's dressing room. I mean, hell, what sense does that make? Men don't care about crap like that. Give it to the women. They are the bulk of the clientele. Usually they are the ones who get the men to try services. The idea is to make the women comfortable."

He lost her at balcony. "There's a balcony?"

"Not in this room. Don't get excited." He inched over until his hand rested on her knee. "Then there's the unisex aspect. To get to the treatment rooms, the women have to pass by the men's waiting room."

“That’s some fabulous planning.”

“Yeah, dumb. I told the owners that many women aren’t comfortable parading around in robes.” His thumb circled her kneecap. “Of course, some are too comfortable.”

“I’m the poster child for the uncomfortable group.”

“Why?”

His cutie factor rose by fifty percent when he showed genuine confusion at her comment.

“Never mind,” she said.

“As if I’d let that comment pass. What did you mean?”

“I’m not exactly thin.”

His eyes narrowed. “Are you kidding?”

“I’m not fat. Just a bit too rounded.” Why in the hell was she talking about this? The more she pointed it out, the more he’d stare at her stomach.

Actually, he’d skipped right from staring to frowning. Great. Highlighting her negatives looked like quite the turn-on.

“Caroline, for a smart woman you’re acting like an ass.” His words didn’t carry any heat. The delivery also came with a sweet little squeeze on her knee.

Whoa. Not the reaction she expected. “I . . . I’m just saying—”

“Stop. You are gorgeous. A tall, stunning redhead with a body that’s kept my dick hard for hours.”

Her stomach tumbled. “Thought you didn’t notice what I looked like without the robe.”

“I know I never said that.” Those fingers found their way under the edge of that robe.

“We were talking about the spa.” That conversation she could handle.

He exhaled loudly. “Women.”

“Men.”

“You’re wrong about your body.” He shook his head.

“Get back to the spa.”

"There are a host of things that could have been done better. Stuff inside the spa and out. It's one of those cases of too much money and not enough thinking."

She wanted to use that quote. "Anything else?"

"Nothing worth bothering you about."

"That's sweet, but—"

His fingertips toured the area right above her knee, tickling with each pass of his forefinger.

"What are you doing?" she asked.

"I'd hoped it would be obvious." The fingers inched higher. Right into flabby territory.

Panic eased away. The sound of his voice worked like a drug, melting all of her resistance and common sense. He faced her now. His head level with her shoulder. His hands up her robe and caressing the outsides of her thighs. His eyes blazing with fire.

Honesty. "I have something to tell you."

"Unless it's about how fast you can take off this robe, I'll wait."

"You don't understand."

"I understand this." Those fingers swept up the inside of her thighs to the hot junction between her legs. He stroked and caressed the soft skin at the very top of her legs.

She tried to stop his hands. "We can't."

"We are."

He pulled her head down and caught her mouth in a hard, possessive kiss. Hands wandering. Hands skimming against bare skin. Fingers wandering across her heat and wetness. His body coaxing and breaking down the firm barrier she placed between work and play.

When they broke apart, a rush of blood thundered in her ears. "I think we should—"

She stopped when she felt the tight knot against her stomach loosen away. The robe fell open, exposing her breasts and stomach.

He finished her sentence. "Get you out of this."

"Alex." His name escaped her lips on a plea.

One hand reached inside her robe and palmed her breast. "Feels like I'm not the only one who is warm."

An understatement. She was on fire.

"Yes," she whispered.

# Chapter Six

Alex weighed his options. There were only two: back out now or enjoy. Relaxing was out of the question. So was continuing with the flirty comebacks. He needed Caroline out of the robe or him out of the room.

She wanted to tell him something. Share some explanation. Not interested. Not now. Pasts and yesterdays didn't matter to him. Never had. He'd been escaping his for too long to hold anyone else to theirs.

He tugged on the edges of the robe to let the material slide off her shoulders and pool on the floor around her. She was rounded and lovely. A real and total woman.

How could this amazing woman look in the mirror and see fat or ugly? Women were strange creatures.

"All I see is a lively, smart, charming and beautiful woman," he mumbled against the base of her throat.

"Where?"

"Under my hands." He trailed a line of kisses right down the center of her chest to her stomach and felt her sharp inhale.

"A little too much beautiful if you ask me."

"That's why I didn't ask you." He licked and kissed, trying to relax her.

"You don't need to say this. It's fine."

But he did. He saw it. For some reason, she missed it. A strong and self-assured woman who obsessed about looking healthy and sexy. The world was a screwed up place.

He rested his hand under her chin. "Know what you need?"

"A wet suit?"

"An exorcism." He lifted her arms out of the robe and pushed the ends off her lap.

"You have much success with that line?"

"The ladies love devil talk."

"You need to find a better class of women."

He already did. "You, Caroline, have demons. And we're going to get rid of the little bastards right now."

With her hands on his ass, she pulled him closer. "I'm not fighting you."

Maybe not with words or by pushing him away, but she was. Some kind of inner battle raged. Something he couldn't see but played a role in. A few seconds ago he would have given in to the lust and not cared. Now he wanted something else.

"You're shielding yourself from me."

"I'm naked."

There was naked and then there was naked. "Let me see you."

"You are."

He placed a hard kiss on her waiting lips. "I see your face, feel your body, but you're hiding."

"I don't know what you're talking about."

"Obviously." He shifted to the side. With his palms on the tile and one quick push, he lifted his body up and out of the pool.

"Very nice."

"Thought you might like that. Been working on it. And, lucky for you, I'm all for live demonstrations."

He stood over her, dripping wet and fully erect. His body

screamed to be inside her. Any other time he would have taken his pleasure and been done. Something about Caroline made him want to be gentle.

"Ready?" he asked. He'd passed ready twenty minutes ago and headed straight for combustion.

Caroline, however, was taking her sweet time. Her gaze traveled up his legs, to his thick erection, then to his face. A shadow of uncertainty moved behind her eyes.

"Going somewhere?" she asked.

"Over there." Before she could protest, he bent down and scooped her up into his arms and out of the shadows. "So are you. I'm not making this journey alone."

"What are you doing?" she asked midyelp.

"Carrying you."

"Good grief, why?"

"I thought the ladies liked romantic gestures like this. Part of the whole tough-guy-who-can-lift-buildings thing." Every step pushed his erection tighter against her hip, making him even harder.

"You forgot the part where the make-believe heroes can cry at the thought of hurt puppies."

"That's ridiculous."

She shrugged those delicious shoulders. "Hey, I don't make the rules."

"For the record, not a fan of people mistreating animals, but no tears. Sorry." Hell, he'd try to cry if he didn't have her soon. That had to count for something on the hero scale.

She shook her head in mock despair. "Another fantasy destroyed."

"We can create a new one."

Every inch of her curled. Her arms around his neck. Her body into his. A sign of cuddling but probably also an issue of hiding. As if she just realized their little chat took place in the nude.

"I guess running laps is part of this fantasy."

The feistiness returned with a vengeance whenever the intimacy got too close. Not sure what to do with that information, he tucked it away for later. "We're walking. In a straight line."

"Silly me."

"Light," he explained.

"Sound," she shot back. "I give up, what are we talking about?"

Despite the tension flowing through his veins, he chuckled. She'd made him laugh more in a few hours than he had in a year. "No more hiding in shadows."

She glanced over his shoulder, then made a production of looking around the room. "Correct me if I'm wrong but the whole area is shadows."

"Except for that sexy candlelit bed you made."

Her mouth fell open, then slammed shut again.

"No arguments?" he asked.

Anxiety hovered at the edge of her gaze. For the first time, something else lingered there, too. A tiny fire that made him believe excitement had finally settled in her head. Perfect.

"I want to see every inch of you," he whispered against her cheek.

"Who am I to argue with a crazy man?"

"That's the spirit."

"If you insist, I'm yours." She bent her back over his arm with as much drama as possible and displayed every inch of those incredible full breasts.

"I do." That was the closest he ever came to saying those words out loud.

With her bundled in his arms, her body gleaming in the soft light, he walked over to the pseudobedding area she'd made earlier. In a slow, measured move, he dropped to his knees with her bundled against his chest. Once there he lowered her to the floor and leaned down, trapping her shoulders between his arms.

All he wanted to do was make love to her. That had to wait one second. "A question."

"Make it fast." She shot him a sly smile just as she dragged her fingernails down his chest to his stomach. "I'm running out of patience."

That made two of them. "Are you married?"

Her fingers stopped their tour of his muscles. "I wouldn't be naked with you if I were married or otherwise committed."

"Good." Great, actually.

"Thanks for the show of faith in asking."

Guilt pricked at him. "Had to make sure."

"Part of that code of yours?"

"The number one rule."

Her hand moved again. This time to wrap around his erection. Somewhere in his haze of lust he realized she hadn't asked about his marital status. Then her hand moved up and down, and he forgot whatever else he planned to say. Kissing her, inviting her to see the amazing woman he saw, was the only goal.

Her deep auburn hair the color of rich red wine spilled over the stark white towels. Her body opened to him and his gaze. Something kicked deep inside his gut.

The wait ended. She'd be his now.

Her hot mouth pressed against his neck. Warm hands caressed his erection and his lower back. Her thighs fell open, making space for him between her legs. Exactly where he wanted to be.

Unable to stand another minute of torment from her soft hands and wet mouth, he grabbed her hands and pinned them over her head. His lips met hers a second later. Kissing, learning her mouth. Her tongue. Her skin.

The warmth of her body penetrated his. Every inch of her

skin, all soft and welcoming, touched his. Fingers twined with fingers. His erection pressed against her moist opening just waiting for the right sign.

She broke off their kiss and dropped her head back against the towels. "Condoms?" she asked on a gasp.

Hearing her over his pants and the beating of his heart wasn't easy, but he made out the words. Then he wanted to rip the spa apart with his bare hands.

"Damn it."

"Alex."

"I don't—"

"Shhh." Her finger touched his lips. "It's okay." Closing her hand over him, she brushed her thumb across his tip and smiled at his groan. "I'm on the pill. I just thought . . ."

The words snapped him back from his fury. "You want to wait? We could just—"

"No. I'm healthy."

His lower half bucked in response to her touches. To the idea of slipping into her bare and letting his body go. "Me, too."

Lips kissed his chin. Then his mouth. "Let's get back to the part where you show me how beautiful I am."

"Let me tell you what I see."

"Showing is fine."

"I need a better view." He fell to his back and pulled her over him.

"Alex!"

"Relax."

Tension pulsed off her shoulders. Rather than sitting up, she crouched against him, as if trying to crawl inside.

"Ride me," he said, half order and half begging.

"Really?"

"Don't think about it. Just do it." His hands smoothed down her back to her lovely butt. With a gentle tug, he pulled her thighs wide until she straddled him.

Ready and excited. That was how he wanted her. He palmed both breasts until her pale shoulders fell and her body melted against his. When the relaxation coursed through her, he took advantage and urged her to sit up.

Those sweet eyes glazed with passion. "Alex, please."

"You know what I see?"

"Tell me," she said in a soft voice.

"Plump breasts, full and mouth-watering." He dropped a kiss on each one.

She moaned but didn't stop him.

"Soft hips and a trim stomach." His fingers dipped into her heat, drawing out her wetness and making her moan.

"Alex—"

"Long, lean legs made for high heels and short skirts." His thumb teased her slit as his finger slipped inside her.

"Don't stop," she said, all breathy and full of need.

"Gorgeous long hair perfect for my fingers. A face that stops my—"

He almost said heart. *What the fuck is that about?*

Her eyes widened. "Make love to me."

A second finger slid up inside of her, opening and preparing her. "Whatever you want."

Her head fell back, sending long auburn hair falling over her shoulders and down behind her. "I want you."

"Take me inside you."

She hummed with excitement. Her body vibrated. The area between her legs creamed. Then she moved.

Holding him in one hand, she readied her body, then slid down on him, inch by slow, burning inch. The feel of her from the inside, all hot and tight and clingy, destroyed the rest of his control. He held her hips, his fingers cupping her flesh, and drew his body deeper into hers. With each plunge, each thrust deep into her and back out again, the pressure inside him built.

All pretense of shyness and self-consciousness disappeared. She rode him without fears or body worries. Her body lifted and fell in time with the breathing pounding from her chest. Thighs tightened against his hips, and inner muscles clamped down on him.

Abandoned and free, so feminine in her ecstasy. Her hair cascaded over those milky white shoulders. A tiny "o" fixed on her swollen mouth as the tension ratcheted up between them.

He wanted to watch her. To see her face as she found her pleasure. To hold her as the clenching rushed through her, speeding to orgasm.

But, he couldn't. He came in a rush, his body giving in to the tremendous tension as he poured into her and pulled her right over the edge with him. As his body bucked, she lifted her body one last time, then screamed his name. On the next clench, she let go, then fell on top of him.

His breathing slowly returned to normal. Having her plastered against his chest, her silky hair covering his arm, gave him a feeling of peace.

Then silence filled the room.

For the first time in a long time, he enjoyed the feeling of nothingness. Of not having to think or prepare. Of just being. His mind blank. The pressures gone.

Then he felt the perspiration on her back. The suffocating heat of the room. Dehydration loomed right around the corner.

Swearing under his breath, he shifted his shoulders and started to sit. "We need to get up."

"Can't move."

A laugh rumbled up his chest. The shaking tossed her around a bit on her perch. "You were moving just fine a second ago."

"Can't talk either."

"You can. For now, but we're too hot."

She lifted her head and smiled down at him. "You mean together?"

"That, too." The smile was infectious. "Temperature is the problem."

"Oh."

"You know what that means."

"No sauna today?"

"Try again."

Her smile vanished. "The dreaded plunge pool."

"Yep."

She slid off his stomach and curled up against his side. "Wait until you see my complaint card on this spa."

With legs like liquid, getting to his feet was a struggle. Not easy at all. "What are you talking about? That was an "A" performance."

She winked at him. "Even higher."

He pulled her up and hugged her to his side. This time she didn't cower or hide. Instead, she walked right by his side, naked and holding his hand.

Progress.

# Chapter Seven

Caroline's body still tingled hours later. Heated lovemaking, followed by a full-body submersion in a cool-water pool, followed by a second lovemaking session on the pool edge led to a very lazy girl.

After all that sexual activity she welcomed the fluffy towel bed and her robe. The candlelight flickered and danced, making shadows on the ceiling. Lying on her back with her robe open and her knees bent, she watched the light show.

"Here you go." Alex dumped a collection of water bottles and power bars on the towels next to her.

Other than the pink towel wrapped around his waist, Alex's nudity matched hers. From his bare feet to his mussed hair he looked good enough to eat. Good thing she didn't have to. "Where did you find the food?"

"On the employee shelves."

"Sounds like an employee violation of some sort." She peeled down the wrapper and dove in. "Is this type of food insubordination tolerated here?"

He gulped back a full bottle of water. "It is now. If I have my way, there will be emergency kits in every room."

"With condoms."

He toasted her with the water bottle. "Damn straight."

The granola bar got worse with each bite. "This tastes like bark."

"Probably is." He handed her a bottle. "Drink. We've been in here for hours. You need to rehydrate."

"Yes, sir."

"Obedience. That's more like it."

Their legs tangled together. The ball of her foot rubbed against his calf. Being away from him, losing contact, seemed unbearable.

"I like this spa."

He popped half of a bar into his mouth. "Does this mean you'll come back?"

The bar dried up in her mouth. "Hmmm?"

"You're here from out of town."

"Yeah." Crumbs caught in her throat.

"From where?"

"All over, really. I travel all the time." That part was true. She hadn't been home in what felt like forever. Why she bothered to pay rent was a mystery.

"Any place you call home?"

"Phoenix."

"More desert."

"I haven't been there for weeks."

"Where have you been and what do you do that takes you away from home?"

"You're chatty all of a sudden." Her toes dipped under his towel. When she moved too high, he held his hand over her foot.

"Thought we needed a sex break."

That made one of them. The change from no action to revved-up-and-ready-to-go happened so fast. All because of him. "I'm a consultant. I go around to different businesses and help assess their strengths and weaknesses."

"Bet they love to see you coming."

Since they didn't know when she was coming, that wasn't an issue. "I was in New York City last week and Miami the week before."

His eyes narrowed. "Really? Where did you stay?"

She rattled off the names of the luxury hotels. "That's part of the reason I wanted the break in the spa. Kind of a cool-down-and-relax thing."

"And how's that working for you?"

"Pretty damn great." No one had invented a word for how great.

"We are a full-service spa here at Berkley, madam," he said in a fake British accent.

"Spanish, right?"

"The heat must be rotting your brain."

"I'm thinking it's the sex."

"Well, maybe we should—"

She leapt a foot off the ground when heavy pounding sounded through the door. Thumping and muffled sounds. Alex's name shouted over and over.

The cavalry had arrived.

Somehow she lost all sense of where they were. The real answer was that she hadn't wanted any connection to the outside world. Now that real life intruded, she resented it.

"Damn!" Alex did some jumping of his own.

"Guess we're rescued."

He stood up and walked over to press his ear against the door. He didn't say much. Mostly listened. She tried to hear, but his responses amounted mostly to "uh-huh" and similar noncommittal boring stuff.

After a few minutes he walked back and loomed over her.

"The lights are back on in the hotel and casino. Everything will come on here in a few minutes."

"That's good." By that she meant terrible.

"Everything is in an uproar. Guests are furious. The staff is pissed." As he spoke, his shoulders stiffened.

She could see the tension take over his body. The lazy relaxation disappeared. Their comfortable companionship vanished in an instant.

"Sounds like a blast," she mumbled back at him.

"If you say so." He got up and tugged on the knot holding the towel together at his waist. The material fell to the floor with a swoosh. "I should have been out of here hours ago."

The words stabbed at her. "You told them to put you last. Your priorities, remember?"

"They never listen to me any other time."

"Time to go?"

"Security will break through in less than ten minutes."

A stray thought moved into her head. "The cameras better be off."

He stopped pulling on his underwear long enough to smile down at her. "They're off."

"That's something."

He shrugged into his tee and shirt and buttoned his sleeves. It was as if she disappeared from his memory with a poof. Something played on his mind. That something didn't appear to be her.

The man could at least wait until she had her clothes on and left the room before forgetting her. "Are you thinking of a way to say 'see you around some time,' because, if so, I can help."

His head shot up. "What?"

"You're getting out of here as if your ass were on fire."

The frowning didn't stop. He just stared at her. And not with a good look.

"Forget it." She turned away.

He turned her right back. With a hand on her arm, he held her still. "Hey. It's not like that."

The contrite, almost sad, look pulling down his mouth helped. Probably saved her from throwing his dry clothes in the pool.

Aiming for nonchalant, she shrugged her shoulders. "That's okay."

"I'm not giving you the kiss-off. I'm trying to get us dressed before those doors open and a security crew of thirty breaks in."

"Did you say thirty?"

"Now that they remembered me, I predict they'll fall over each other trying to please me. There are talks of downsizing around here. Losing the assistant manager during a crisis could be seen as a career killer."

"Downsizing?" The work part of her brain kicked into gear again.

"Doesn't matter. No one is going to get in trouble."

"Because you're a good guy."

"Because I didn't care about being rescued."

Her heart did a little flip. "Why not?"

"I was too busy being seduced by a lovely lady." He kissed her then. Those lips warming her from the inside out. Again. Just as she wanted.

She looped her arms around his neck. "I do like your whatever-the-guest-wants attitude."

She was kidding, but he took the comment seriously. "It's never happened before."

"What are we talking about?"

"You. The only guest I've ever slept with."

She pulled back to get a good look at those baby blues. "Really?"

"Just you." One last kiss on her nose. "Now, get dressed or I'll parade you through the halls looking like that."

* * *

He skipped the parade but did insist on walking her back to her room. Fully dressed with a robe tucked under her arm, she stood at the door ready to say goodbye.

"I know you have work to do," she said before slipping her card key out of her pocket. "You don't have to baby-sit me."

"Maybe I want to kiss you senseless and think doing that in the hall is a bad idea." He took the key and slid it into the lock.

"I like your management style."

"Happy to be of service."

Everything about this man felt right. She tried to remember the last time a guy made her laugh. "Would you like to come in for a nightcap?"

"It's morning, and drinking is the last thing on my mind." Pushing the door open, he gestured her inside the deluxe room.

"Sweet talker."

Just inside the door he spun her around. The robe fell out of her arms and to the plush blue carpeting along with her notebook. With her back pressed against the door and her arms hugging his shoulders, he kissed her. Hands roamed freely over her face and breasts while his lips worked magic on her mouth.

Between the hard door behind her and the even harder body in front of her, she lost control. Want and need mixed together. Common sense evaporated.

She judged the distance from the door to the king-sized canopy bed. Maybe ten feet. They could make it.

When she reached for his belt, he stopped her. Again. This was getting to be a habit.

"Wait." He broke off the kiss and rested his forehead against the door.

"What?"

His head didn't move. "Damn. I can't."

She squeezed his erection through his pants. "I bet you can."

"Hell, yeah, I can. It's—"

She knew the answer. "Work."

"Work," he repeated back.

"I suddenly hate your work ethic."

"You're not alone." He raised his head and stared down at her. The need was visible in his blue eyes.

"You're going to leave." The words tasted sour in her mouth.

He slid his hands down her sides to her waist. "Got to."

"Okay." He hadn't even left yet, and already the idea was anything but okay.

"I'll be back," he said.

Ahhh. The line passed from father to son for generations. The same line that tormented decades of women who fell for those stupid men.

"Of course."

His eyebrow lifted. "I'm serious."

Serious but still leaving. "Uh-huh."

"Tell me how long you're staying at Berkley."

So they could fit in another quickie or two. "You don't have to—"

"I can check the computer, but coughing up the information will be faster."

A quickie or two was better than nothing. "A few more days."

"Good." He nodded. "I'll be back in a few hours."

"I'll be here." She'd never been there for anyone in her life. Would he even want her there if he knew about her?

"Keep the bed warm for me." He kissed her one last long, lingering time.

"We're going to try a bed this time? That would be new."

"You'll need this." He turned to drop the card on the table and scooped up her notebook on the way.

He threw the haul on the table and took one step toward her before stopping. His smile faded as he turned back and away from her. With his palms flat against the table, he leaned down and studied something—

No! She couldn't be that unlucky.

"Alex!"

She reached him right as he turned around to face her. "What the hell is this?"

The "this" in question was a copy of her assignment memo, complete with jabs and jokes from her boss all at Berkley's expense. The same document that outlined the parameters of her review. The same one crumpled into a wad in his fist.

"Nothing. Work." She tried to grab it back.

He raised his arm to keep her away. "You're Veronica Hampton? You?"

Lying wouldn't work here. He'd found what there was to find. The evidence of her fake identity. The one everyone in his business knew. Nothing could fix this.

She felt every drop of blood drain from her face. "I'm Caroline Rogers."

"Caroline," he warned.

"Veronica doesn't exist."

"Let's stop with the verbal games." He shook the papers in front of her face. "This is you. You're the reviewer. The woman who goes around and finds fault in everything."

She couldn't accept that. He may hate her and her job, but she deserved respect. "I review hotels."

"You rip them apart."

"Only when they deserve it."

"And now it's Berkley's turn?" He motioned as if he were going to throw the wadded-up ball at the bed, then changed his mind.

"I came here to—"

"Save it." He raised both hands, just as he did when they first met. Only this time, the gesture wasn't soothing.

The need to touch him overwhelmed her. She wanted to give comfort and reassurance. She reached out and let her hand slide down his tie to his waist. "Let me explain."

"No thanks." He stepped back from her touch. "I'll wait to read it in the article."

Then he left. And she felt nothing.

# Chapter Eight

He barely got the door closed and into the hallway before retrieving her small notebook from his jacket pocket. The leather-bound pad shook in his hands. Scanning her notes, it all fell into place. All the travel. The high-end hotel stays. The comments about grades on the hotel. Hell, he'd read the review on the Miami resort already. Blistering. Vicious.

Shit . . . he'd told her stuff. Inside, private stuff. Stuff that shouldn't go in a review or article.

Scammed. Great sex, but still conned. Not so much by the fact the infamous Veronica the Bitch and Caroline Rogers were one and the same. By everything else. Come to his hotel, collect information and do her job. Fine. Sleep with him and look up at him with those soft doe eyes. That fucking sucked.

"Screw me? Screw her."

He shoved the notepad into his pocket and stalked down the hall. He got the whole way to the elevator, getting hotter with each step. Jammed the down button six times. Then a seventh. Then stopped.

He couldn't leave it like this. He had to know.

No way she'd let him back in. She got what she wanted. Game over for Caroline, or whatever the hell her name was.

Time to use the manager passkey. He could get in any room at any time, so long as the electricity was up and running. There was only one room he wanted to get in.

He stormed back down the hall and stopped at Caroline's room. After one sharp knock, he slipped the card into the lock and threw open the door. He nearly flattened her. She stood right on the other side. Despite his anger, his reflexes were intact. He caught the edge right before it slammed into her side.

"Alex? What are you doing?"

"We have to talk."

She took a step back. "I was coming to find you."

"For an interview, I guess. No thanks." He didn't feel very charitable, so every word came out as a snap.

"To talk."

"Didn't you get everything you needed? Any other inside information you want me to spill?"

"Our time in the spa didn't have anything to do with the report."

He scoffed. "You can't be serious."

"They were separate things."

He wanted to believe her but refused. "You can't think I'm that stupid."

"You're pigheaded."

The more he shouted, the calmer she got.

"I'm pissed, Caroline. We spent the entire evening together and you failed to mention who you really are. You owe me an explanation."

"I expected you to come back with security and kick me out." She looked at him with a glassy, distant look in her eyes.

"So you could have something else to write about? How dumb do you think I am? Forget that. I know the answer. Pretty damn dumb."

Sadness passed behind her eyes. She looked down for a

second, but by the time she returned his gaze again, the cloud disappeared. "I'll explain everything if you'll listen."

Need crashed against him. Seeing her look so vulnerable wore him down. "Start."

"I work for Hotel and Tourism. My next review is on Berkley."

Hearing her say it in a flat, calm voice stole some of his anger. That was the job part. He didn't like it, but he understood it. You get an assignment, you do it. The rest of it was the problem.

"Go on," he said.

"There's nothing else to tell."

"Like hell." He closed the door and turned the lock. "Get to the part about the spa and me."

She pulled back as if he'd slapped her. "I told you. What happened in the spa had nothing to do with the review."

"So I won't be graded on my sexual skills?" Anger sharpened his words.

She closed her eyes briefly. "Alex, I know you're mad but don't be stupid."

"Is that your apology?"

"I snuck into the spa to check it out. Once there, I decided to sample the facilities. I didn't have any control over the lights, the electricity or you."

All that made sense. He didn't want it to, but it did. The rest of his confusion faded away. Desire settled in its place. He wanted this woman. Despite everything, he wanted her.

Her voice softened into a gentle plea. "You're looking for some grand conspiracy. You won't find it. I didn't set you up, Alex. You appeared."

"Seems convenient."

"Trust me, you are anything but convenient." She gave him a sad smile, then walked over and plunked herself on the edge of the bed. "There are two jobs on the line here. Mine means as much to me as yours does to you."

He appreciated her dedication to work. It was everything else she did and said, none of it real, that ate at his gut. "Why the lying?"

"I didn't lie. I told you what I did. I tried to tell you exactly what I did. You didn't want to know. Do you have any idea how many times I've broken my confidential cover? Never. Not once. Only for you."

Every word chipped away at the shield he'd erected against her. Devotion to work. Responsibility. The pieces fit. And he did cut her off when she tried to explain.

"Alex, be honest. You were as eager to avoid history and the past as I was. We both wanted here and now."

He knew it was the truth the minute she said the words. She ran from her past just like he did. They both had something to hide and something to overcome. It shaped them. Wounded them, maybe.

But he was so tired of running. He loved his job. Had a good life. Up until yesterday all that was sufficient. After a night trapped with her, he knew there was something else out there. Healthy companionship. Emotions he tried to ignore. Passion that made him wild.

He waited for the usual feelings of panic. For the urge to push her away to settle in. For the anxiety he felt whenever a woman got too close to hit him. The opposite happened. Instead of anxiety, he felt a pulsing need.

Something brewed between them. Something he had to explore and nurture. And he had to convince Caroline that the something was worth working on.

They were less than five feet apart, yet she felt all alone. He had fallen silent. Contemplating. Probably figuring out how to ditch her in the desert and hide all evidence of her existence.

She never planned for this to happen. She came for a job. The idea was to do some work, have some fun. Move on.

Making love with him was spectacular, so freeing and open. It shouldn't have been anything more.

Her life should have shifted right back into place as soon as her breathing returned to normal. It didn't. Everything felt wrong. Out of place.

For the first time in her adult life she had allowed the lines between work and pleasure to blur. Work took a back-seat. Was her last priority. It all scared the hell out of her.

Part of her wanted to run out of Vegas. The other wanted to stay right there and explore whatever it was she had with Alex. That had never happened before. She wondered if it could ever happen again.

All she knew was that she wanted it to happen with him. That meant sacrifice. Asking headquarters for a replacement due to her conflict of interest. An act like that would set her career path back a bit. Would create a tie. And she really couldn't afford any of those.

Without warning he sat down next to her on the bed. The scent of eucalyptus clung to him. This time, the smell didn't make her sick.

"You have a decision to make," he said.

Little did he know. "How do you figure?"

"Your identity has been a secret. You're very good. Without walking you back here and seeing the stash of materials on your table, I never would have put it together."

"It's part of my job. A big part."

"I wonder if you would have told me or walked out."

"I don't know." She stared down at her hands until he lifted her chin with his fingertips. "I tried to tell you, but I thought the moment passed. That you would get back to work and . . ."

"Yeah?"

She shifted so she could look in his eyes. "Veronica isn't me. She's what I do. I know it's easy to confuse the two."

"Ahh, that." He sat, elbows on knees, and tapped his fingertips together. "I know what I need to know about Caroline Rogers."

"That she's a liar?"

"She's beautiful. Smart. Dedicated. Hard worker. Likes to travel. Loves the spa. Flawed but not in the ways she thinks she is. In ways that linger deep inside, but none of that makes her any less amazing."

"Alex, I'm serious."

"So am I."

He needed to understand who she really was. What drove her. "My work is my life."

"That's where you're wrong. Your life is your life. Work is a part of who you are but only a piece."

His explanation sounded so normal. She wished it were that simple. "Not for me."

"Up until last night, not for me either. But I'm suggesting we both change our priorities."

"I'm not the settle-down type. You aren't either."

"Does trying out a commitment to another person mean settling?"

She knew only one way. He wanted her to think about another. The idea made her insides jump with excitement even as her brain screamed for her to run. "It always has."

"Running and hiding are different from being smart."

"I'm not hiding."

"You are in every way that matters." He twined his fingers through hers. "You can have it all if you want to try."

He was offering life and love. Everything she wanted but didn't deserve. "Meaning?"

"No one appreciates commitment to work more than I do. But, there has to be more. You have to stop moving sometime. Find a place to call home and a person to come home to."

"Don't let the age fool you. I've been on the move a long time."

"You're not alone."

"Tell me." She wanted to know. Wanted to experience what he'd experienced and wipe the past clean.

For a minute or two he stayed quiet. When he spoke, his voice was low and soft. "Running from a past that embarrassed me. From poverty that sickened me. From desperation that infuriated me."

"Alex—"

"I'm not asking for pity. I survived, but when is enough, enough? We can have something else. Something better."

Light and something that felt like hope washed through her. He understood. He wasn't just saying the words. He'd lived it. He knew. Getting in her panties or wooing her with fancy words and smooth moves wasn't the goal.

Deep down, they both came from the same place. A bad place. Maybe it was time to find a good place. Together.

"What are you suggesting?"

A smile wiped that serious look right off his face. "A chance. Try a different desert. Trade Phoenix and a home you never visit for Las Vegas and a guy to come home to."

Excitement and happiness bubbled up inside her. She realized the satisfaction she'd experienced before Alex wasn't good enough. Now she wanted to squeal and scream with joy.

She tamped down on those feelings, tried to stay calm until she got her concerns on the table. "I travel. A lot. It's part of who I am."

"I'm not trying to change you, Caroline. Travel, but come back to me." He lifted their bound hands to his mouth and kissed the back of her hand.

"Yes," she said on a sigh.

"I'll take Caroline and Veronica, and anyone else you have in there."

"There's just me, and I'm a one-man gal." A woman falling and not minding the absence of a net for the first time in her life.

"Then it's a good thing my priorities are in order." He pushed her back onto the bed and hovered over her.

She wrapped her arms around his neck. "Where do I fit on that list?"

"At the very top." He nuzzled her throat. "We're two of a kind, honey. You top my list and I'll top yours."

She pulled his shirt out of his pants. "I'll let you know tomorrow."

"What happens tomorrow?"

She dragged the material up and over his back until all she could feel was soft, smooth skin. "Come on, I'm a professional. I can't give you a thorough review after only one night."

"We can't have that."

"This could take weeks."

"Months." He lifted his hips and stripped off his shirt and tee.

Her fingers found his belt. "Years."

"Think I'll make the grade?" he asked with a mischievous smile.

"You already have."

Here's a scintillating look at
Sylvia Day's
ASK FOR IT.
Available now from Brava!

George looked easily over her head to scrutinize the scene. "I say. It appears Lord Westfield is heading this way."

"Are you quite certain, Mr. Stanton?"

"Yes, my lady. Westfield is staring directly at me as we speak."

Tension coiled in the pit of her stomach. Marcus had literally frozen in place when their eyes had first met and the second glance had been even more disturbing. He was coming for her and she had no time to prepare. George looked down at her as she resumed fanning herself furiously.

*Damn Marcus for coming tonight*! Her first social event after three years of mourning and he unerringly sought her out within hours of her reemergence, as if he'd been impatiently waiting these last years for exactly this moment. She was well aware that that had not been the case at all. While she had been crepe-clad and sequestered in mourning, Marcus had been firmly establishing his scandalous reputation in many a lady's bedroom.

After the callous way he'd broken her heart, Elizabeth would have discounted him regardless of the circumstances but tonight especially. Enjoyment of the festivities was not her aim. She had a man she was waiting for, a man she had arranged covertly to meet. Tonight she would dedicate herself to the memory of her husband. She would find justice for Hawthorne and see it served.

The crowd parted reluctantly before Marcus and then regrouped in his wake, the movements heralding his progress toward her. And then Westfield was there, directly before her. He smiled and her pulse raced. The temptation to retreat, to flee, was great, but the moment when she could reasonably have done so passed far too swiftly.

Squaring her shoulders, Elizabeth took a deep breath. The glass in her hand began to tremble and she quickly swallowed the whole of its contents to avoid spilling on her dress. She passed the empty vessel to George without looking. Marcus caught her hand before she could retrieve it.

Bowing low with a charming smile, his gaze never broke contact with hers. "Lady Hawthorne. Ravishing, as ever." His voice was rich and warm, reminding her of crushed velvet. "Would it be folly to hope you still have a dance available, and that you would be willing to dance it with me?"

Elizabeth's mind scrambled, attempting to discover a way to refuse. His wickedly virile energy, potent even across the room, was overwhelming in close proximity.

"I am not in attendance to dance, Lord Westfield. Ask any of the gentlemen around us."

"I've no wish to dance with them," he said dryly, "so their thoughts on the matter are of no consequence to me."

She began to object when she perceived the challenge in his eyes. He smiled with devilish amusement, visibly daring her to proceed, and Elizabeth paused. She would not give him the satisfaction of thinking she was afraid to dance with him. "You may claim this next set, Lord Westfield, if you insist."

He bowed gracefully, his gaze approving. He offered his arm and led her toward the dance floor. As the musicians began to play and music rose in joyous swell through the room, the beautiful strains of the minuet began.

Turning, Marcus extended his arm toward her. She placed her hand atop the back of his, grateful for the gloves that separated their skin. The ballroom was ablaze with candles, which cast him in golden light and brought to her attention the strength of his shoulder as it flexed. Lashes lowered, she appraised him for signs of change.

Marcus had always been an intensely physical man, engaging in a variety of sports and activities. Impossibly, it appeared he had grown stronger, more formidable. He was power personified and Elizabeth marveled at her past naiveté in believing she could tame him. Thank God, she was no longer so foolish.

His one softness was his luxuriously rich brown hair. It shone like sable and was tied at the nape with a simple black ribbon. Even his emerald gaze was sharp, piercing with a fierce intelligence. He had a clever mind to which deceit was naught but a simple game, as she had learned at great cost to her heart and pride.

She had half expected to find the signs of dissipation so common to the indulgent life and yet his handsome face bore no such witness. Instead he wore the sun-kissed appearance of a man who spent much of his time outdoors. His nose was straight and aquiline over lips that were full and sensuous. At the moment those lips were turned up on one side in a half smile that was at once boyish and alluring. He remained perfectly gorgeous from the top of his head to the soles of his feet. He was watching her studying him, fully aware that she could not help but admire his handsomeness. She lowered her eyes and stared resolutely at his jabot.

The scent that clung to him enveloped her senses. It was a wonderfully manly scent of sandalwood, citrus, and Marcus's own unique essence. The flush of her skin seeped into her insides, mingling with her apprehension.

Reading her thoughts, Marcus tilted his head toward her. His voice, when it came, was low and husky. "Elizabeth. It is a long-awaited pleasure to be in your company again."

"The pleasure, Lord Westfield, is entirely yours."

"You once called me Marcus."

"It would no longer be appropriate for me to address you so informally, my lord."

His mouth tilted into a sinful grin. "I give you leave to be inappropriate with me at any time you choose. In fact, I have always relished your moments of inappropriateness."

"You have had a number of willing women who suited you just as well."

"Never, my love. You have always been separate and apart from every other female."

Elizabeth had met her share of scoundrels and rogues but always their slick confidence and overtly intimate manners left her unmoved. Marcus was so skilled at seducing women, he managed the appearance of utter sincerity. She'd once believed every declaration of adoration and devotion that had fallen from his lips. Even now, the way he looked at her with such fierce longing seemed so genuine she almost believed it.

He made her want to forget what kind of man he was—a heartless seducer. But her body would not let her forget. She felt feverish and faintly dizzy.

Take a peek at Diane Whiteside's
THE SOUTHERN DEVIL.
Coming next month from Brava. . . .

The mantel clock began to chime.

Jessamyn's head flashed around to stare at it before she looked back at Morgan.

She forced back her body's awareness of him. "I needed him as my husband, you fool! For two hours, starting now."

"Husband?" Jealousy swept over his face.

"In a lawyer's office," she snarled back. "I have to be there with a husband in fifteen minutes, or all is lost. Damn you, let me go!"

The clock chimed again.

His eyes narrowed for a moment, then he pulled her up to him. His grip was less painful but just as inescapable as before. "A bargain then, Jessamyn. I'll play your husband for a few hours, if you'll join me in a private parlor for the same span of time afterward."

She gasped. A devil's bargain, indeed.

"Nine years ago, before you married Cyrus, I promised you revenge for what you did, and you agreed my claim was just. Two hours won't see that accomplished but it's a start," he purred, his drawl knife-edged and laced with carnal promise.

Her flight or fight instincts stirred, honed by seven years

as an Army wife on the bloody Kansas prairies. She reined them in sternly: No matter how angry he'd been, surely Morgan would never harm a woman, no matter what preposterous demands he'd hurled nine years ago when she'd held him captive.

Her fingers bit into his arms, as she tried to think of another option. But if she didn't appear with a husband, she'd lose her only chance of regaining Somerset Hall, her family's old home . . .

The mantel clock sounded the third, and last, note.

She agreed to his bargain, the words like ashes in her throat. "Very well, Morgan. Now will you take me across the street to the lawyer's?"

Morgan escorted Jessamyn across the street with all the haughtiness his father would have shown escorting his mother aboard a riverboat. It was a bit of manners ingrained in him so early that he didn't need to think about it, something he'd first practiced with Jessamyn when she was five and their parents first openly hoped for a wedding between them. Such an ingrained habit was very useful when his brain seemed to have dived somewhere south of his belt buckle as soon as she'd agreed she owed him revenge.

What was he going to do first? There were so many activities he'd learned in Consortium houses, of how to drive a woman insane with desire. How to leave her sated and panting, willing to do anything to repeat the experience. More than anything else, he needed to see Jessamyn aching to be touched by him again and again.

A black curl stroked her cheek in just the way he planned to later. He smiled, planning, and reached for the office door.

*Ebenezer Abercrombie & Sons, Attys. At Law* announced the sturdy letters on its surface.

Morgan stiffened. Her lawyer was that Abercrombie? Halpern's friend and Millicent's godfather, who Morgan had dined with last night? Who'd beamed approval as Halpern and his wife had shoved Morgan at their daughter and he'd made no mention of a wife?

Damn, damn, damn.

Jessamyn, who'd never been a fool, caught his momentary hesitation and glanced up at him.

He shook his head slightly at her and put his hand on the door knob. Suddenly it turned under his fingers and swung open to frame Abercrombie's well-fed bulk. The man's eyes widened briefly as he took in both of his visitors.

Jessamyn leaned closer to Morgan and squeezed his arm, with all the assurance of a long-married woman. God knows he'd seen her do it with Cyrus before.

Morgan shifted himself so she could fit comfortably, as he'd seen his cousin do. She settled easily within a hand's-breadth of him and tilted her head at Abercrombie expectantly. The entire byplay took only a few seconds.

The lawyer's eyes narrowed and his mouth tightened before a polite professional mask covered his face. "Good afternoon, Evans. What an unexpected pleasure to see you here today."

Morgan smiled with all the smooth charm he'd polished as one of Bedford Forrest's spies. "The pleasure is entirely mine, Abercrombie. I've the honor of escorting my wife. Jessamyn, my dear, have you met Mr. Abercrombie?" He could have kicked himself. His Mississippi drawl was slightly heavier than usual, a telltale sign of nervousness. Jessamyn took Abercrombie's hand, with all the charm of her aristocratic Memphis upbringing. "Yes, Mr. Abercrombie was my uncle's lawyer for years. I've known him since I was a child. Hello, sir."

Abercrombie kissed her cheek. "My dear lady, I'm so

glad you were able to bring your husband." His eyes flickered to Morgan but his countenance was impassive. "Your cousin Charles and his wife are seated in my office, waiting for the reading of the will to begin. Please come with me."

Here's "In Bad With Someone"
by Rosemary Laurey
in the upcoming anthology,
TEXAS BAD BOYS.
Available next month from Brava!

Anger, shock and a touch of fury propelled Rod across the road with just a quick "Gotta go!" to his buddies. He pushed open the door and looked around *his* bar. What the hell was Mary-Beth playing at? The two suits were getting ready to leave. Maude Wilson and her cronies were playing rummy as they did most afternoons, practicing character assassination as they bet for nickel points. The only other occupant was the sharp-looking redhead he'd noticed earlier walking up Center Street.

Her perky little butt was poised on one of the counter stools while she ate . . . he walked closer . . . a burger and onion rings. A bacon burger with Swiss.

Cold rage at Pete's double-dealing clenched Rod's gut. Still not quite believing. Suspecting some twisted joke, Rod met Mary-Beth's eyes. She shifted them sideways to the redhead.

Shit!

Okay, deep breath here. He could hardly yank her lovely butt off the stool and slug her one. His mama had taught him better than that but dammit, what did she think she was doing claiming his bar as her own? Might as well find out.

Giving Mary-Beth a warning glance to stay cool, he took

the stool nearest Madame Bar Snatcher. "Hey, there Mary-Beth. How about pulling me a nice, cold beer."

"I'm sorry. Excuse me," the redhead said and moved her pocket book, giving him a glimpse of deep, green eyes before she turned back to her onion rings, cut one in four, stabbed it with the fork and chewed carefully.

Snob and prissy wasn't in it! Nice boobs though. Not that it was likely to do him any good. Her hair was something else though: the color of new pennies, and cut short in a mass of curls. He itched to reach out and let a strand of hair curl over his fingers. Pity it came with a bar snatcher attached.

"Here you are, Rod." Mary-Beth set his glass down with a thud . . . and a smirk. "Anything else I can get you?"

"Fine thanks. This is just what I need."

She rolled her eyes and proceeded to refill Miss Prissy's ice water. What exactly Mary-Beth had done to earn that wide smile he'd like to know, but it did enable him to catch Miss Prissy's eye.

"Howdy!"

"Good afternoon," she replied, with a little nod.

"Enjoying Silver Gulch?" he asked before she had a chance to chop up another onion ring.

She paused as if weighing up whether to snub him or not. "It's interesting. Smaller than I imagined but . . ." She gave him the oddest look as her mouth twitched at the corner. "Definitely fascinating."

"Here on a visit or just passing through town?" He asked, nicely casual, as he lifted his glass and took a drink.

She smiled, almost chuckled. Her green eyes crinkling at the corners as she looked him in the eye. "I'll be staying, Mr. Carter."

Rod almost spluttered his Hefeweizen all over himself and the counter. He grabbed his handkerchief and wiped his mouth, thanking heaven he didn't have beer running out of his nose. Damn her! Damn the smug little smirk on her pretty face! And double damn Mary-Beth for setting him up like this!

"It wasn't Mary-Beth, so don't give her the evil eye like that."

Read minds could she? "How did you know who I was?"

"An educated guess, Mr. Carter. Gabe Rankin told me your name. Minutes after I identify myself to Mary-Beth you appear off the street where you were chatting. How many 'Rods' are there in a town this size?" While he digested that, she held out a slim, long-fingered hand. "I'm Juliet ffrench. My grandfather left me this building and the business."

"We'll see about that!"

He felt her green eyes watching him as he stormed out. Gabe Rankin had some explaining to do.

After twenty minutes cooling his heels to see Gabe and an acrimonious ten minutes face to face, Rod learned old man Maddock had done him dirty and given away the Rooster from under his feet.

"We had a deal!" Rod protested.

"I know you did," Gabe replied, shaking his head. "He knew it too. Said he had only three parcels of property and they had to go to his granddaughters. Said he'd make it right with you."

But the old codger had upended his fishing boat before he could. "So what now? I get kicked out after building up the business?"

"Now, calm down, Rod," Gabe went on. "It's not too bad. Part of the agreement was Mizz ffrench keep on all the employees." So he was an employee now was he? "If you ask me, she'll not hang around long, whatever she's saying right now. You mark my words, give it a couple of months and she'll be back in London and you'll be running the Rooster just like always."

Not quite like always. He'd no longer be working for himself but prissy Mizz ffrench. "What if I just quit?" There was an idea!

Gabe waved his hands palms outermost and shook his head. "Now don't you start making hasty decisions, Rod. Why not bide your time and see how things go? The Rooster wouldn't be the same without you." It would not be anything without him and Gabe damn well knew it. "You just hold on a week or two. See how things work out between you and Miss ffrench.

Fat lot of help Gabe was.

Rod was even more steamed when he walked back into the Rooster, ready to hash out a few details with the new owner.

Who wasn't there.

Neither was Mary-Beth. Lucas, the cook, was standing in at the bar. Where the hell were they? Off doing each other's hair? And he'd been stupid enough to think Mary-Beth was on his side.

"Don't look so sour, boss," Lucas said.

"Where the hell is Mary-Beth? She's got two more hours of her shift."

"She took the new owner on the tour. Say, is she really old man Maddock's granddaughter?"

"Yes, Rod, we were wondering that." Old Maude and her cronies swooped on him like the furies. "Is it true? And Pete left her the Rooster. How nice!"

It wasn't nice and it got worse. Two days later, Juliet ffrench had settled in. There was no stopping her.

She could have stayed in the comparative comfort of Sally Jones's B &B, or even the Hunting Lodge just outside town, but Miss ffrench insisted on moving in. Since the other apartments were boarded up and uninhabitable, she moved into his. After a night on the lumpy sofa, she drove into Pebble Creek and the next morning, carpet and furniture were delivered and she spent the afternoon hanging drapes and unpacking as she staked her claim on one of the empty rooms. His final objection that there was only one functioning bathroom, was met with a bland smile and the unblinking assurance not to worry, she promised not to use his razor to shave her legs.

A weaker man would have given up.

Rod Carter braced for survival. He'd outlast Juliet ffrench and be a gentleman about it.